BLOOD ROSE

IN THE SHADOWS - BOOK 8

P. T. MICHELLE

LIMITLESS INK PRESS

BLOOD ROSE

IN THE SHADOWS - BOOK 8

In the Shadows Series
Reading Order

Mister Black (Book 1 - Talia & Sebastian, Part 1)
Scarlett Red (Book 2 - Talia & Sebastian, Part 2)
Blackest Red (Book 3 - Talia & Sebastian, Part 3)
Gold Shimmer (Book 4 - Cass & Calder, Part 1)
Steel Rush (Book 5 - Cass & Calder, Part 2)
Black Platinum (Book 6 - Talia & Sebastian, Stand Alone Novel)
Reddest Black (Book 7 - Talia & Sebastian, Stand Alone Novel)
Blood Rose (Book 8 - Cass & Calder, Stand Alone Novel)
Noble Brit (Book 9 - Mina & Den, Stand Alone Novel - Coming March 2019)

Note: Mister Black is the only novella. All the other books are novel length.

DEAR READERS: *The* ***In the Shadows*** *series must be read in the following order:* ***MISTER BLACK***, ***SCARLETT RED***, *and* ***BLACKEST RED***. *Sebastian and Talia's happy-ever-after is contained within books 1-3. Cass and Calder's epic love story follows in books 4-5 with* ***GOLD SHIMMER*** *and* ***STEEL RUSH***. *Be sure to read books 4-5, since you'll also get to visit with Sebastian and Talia as they play key roles in Cass and Calder's story. The rest of the books in the series:* ***BLACK PLATINUM, REDDEST BLACK, BLOOD ROSE,*** *and* ***NOBLE BRIT*** *are all stand alone novels.*

When you find that person who gets you,
never let them go!

COPYRIGHT

Print ISBN-13: 9781939672438
Print ISBN-10: 1939672430

To stay informed when the next P.T. Michelle book will be released, join P.T. Michelle's free newsletter http://bit.ly/11tqAQN.

Cover credit: Cover designed by P.T. Michelle
V07122018

SUMMARY

Calder Blake lost everything: his mother, his father, his very identity. Until Cass, he didn't believe he deserved to be a Blake, where family and loyalty always come first.

But what if Cass can't give Calder what he needs to move on from his broken past?

Or worse, what if someone's determined that Cass will never get a chance to become a Blake?

*Dear Readers: **BLOOD ROSE** is a stand alone story, but if you haven't read how Cass and Calder's love story first started, you can do so through **GOLD SHIMMER** and **STEEL RUSH**. Not only do you get to take the journey with Cass and Calder, but you'll also get to visit with Sebastian and Talia, since they play key roles in Cass and Calder's story. :)*

IN THE SHADOWS SERIES:

Mister Black (Book 1 - Talia & Sebastian, Part 1)
Scarlett Red (Book 2 - Talia & Sebastian, Part 2)
Blackest Red (Book 3 - Talia & Sebastian, Part 3)
Gold Shimmer (Book 4 - Cass & Calder, Part 1)
Steel Rush (Book 5 - Cass & Calder, Part 2)
Black Platinum (Book 6 - Talia & Sebastian, Stand Alone Novel)
Reddest Black (Book 7 - Talia & Sebastian, Stand Alone Novel)
Blood Rose (Book 8 - Cass & Calder, Stand Alone Novel)
Noble Brit (Book 9 - Mina & Den, Stand Alone Novel - Coming March 2019)

CHAPTER ONE

CASS

Library.

I stare at the text message that pops up on my phone just as Beth Carver disappears inside the restaurant to say hello to a friend from college who's the bistro's chef. It's the second time I received the same text from a blocked number. I assumed the first one was sent to me by mistake, but the timing—I check the timestamp, because I've had some issues with delayed messages—while I'm having lunch with Beth Carver, suddenly gives the repeated message a whole other meaning.

Goose bumps form on my arms despite the summer sun warming my skin. I tense my jaw and quickly glance around Bistro Café's outdoor seating and across the busy street, using all the skills my investigator best friend Talia taught me about taking in a scene. As I walked to the restaurant from the train, I'd glanced over my shoulder a couple of times. I couldn't shake the feeling I was being followed. I hadn't tied it to that stupid first text, but now... I'm not so sure. My fingers flex to grab my camera sitting on the table, but that would be too obvious. I turn my head casually and scan for a woman around my age with similar height and body shape. She'll be wearing a wig, or hat, and likely sunglasses to hide her identity. But I know Celeste Carver's appearance better than anyone. As my doppelgänger twin, she might have my face and dark hair, but we don't share an ounce of DNA. No, her familial tie belongs to the girl with light-brown hair who just went inside.

Beth thinks her big sister, Celeste, was murdered by her father's psychopath business partner Phillip Hemming. And here I sit, forced to keep Celeste's secret from the world and her family while trying to be a friend to Beth.

Guilt is a powerful motivator.

Phillip's betrayal to the Carver family was absolutely jail-worthy, but thanks to Celeste duping me into pretending to be her for one evening, I'd unwittingly played a part in helping her frame the man for her murder. While Celeste disappeared with her unborn child Phillip had fathered to guarantee his piece of the Carver fortune, I was left to convince the police that I wasn't actually Celeste and had nothing to do with her disappearance.

In my brief time in the Carver household, I grew to really like Beth. She deserves to know the truth, but Celeste's tapestry of lies were too intricately woven, and if I tugged on even one thread to reveal the true color underneath, the whole picture could unravel, destroying many lives with it, including mine.

I'd hoped this lunch with Beth would distract me from my own worries about my future with Calder, but the possibility that Celeste might be back after over a year of silence is the last kind of distraction I need.

Annoyed that some random text is freaking me out, I quickly type a response.

Wrong number.

Just as I set my phone down, a movement in my periphery draws my attention to the woman sitting alone at a table near the corner. The wind blowing around the building's edge is flapping her wide-brimmed hat, forcing her to fold it toward her face to keep it in place. Her build is right. Manicured nails. Entitled air and perfect posture. As she looks at her phone, then lifts it toward her face, my heart races.

I zero on her jawline just beyond her hat's brim. *Turn so I can see you.*

My phone's sudden ring jacks my racing pulse.

I'm torn between keeping my line of sight on her or looking at my phone's display.

Holding my breath, I blindly grab my phone just as the woman looks up.

It's not her. *Stop being paranoid, Cass.* I exhale my relief and quickly look down to see Calder on my Caller ID.

"Where are you?" he says in a tense tone the moment I answer. "Talia said you were coming to the office. I wanted to take you to lunch."

"Beth called at the last minute so we're grabbing lunch. I'm popping by the office to drop off the photos for Talia, then I have a business meeting. I'm sorry, Calder."

"What business meeting? Your other picture book isn't due for six months."

My fingers tighten around my phone. "I do have other things going on."

"Has Talia given you more work? Why didn't she tell me? Why the hell am I Sebastian's business partner if I'm the last to know about half the shit going on around here?"

I frown at the tension in his voice. "Why are you so grumbly?"

"Hemming is here."

"Whether you like it or not, Ben's a part of BLACK Security. We talked about you trying with him."

"I have a vague recollection of you mentioning it. I

was too busy watching your gorgeous mouth and thinking about all the things I've yet to do with it."

He always gets to me. Even over the phone that sexy voice makes me melt. Even when I'm trying to make a point. I ignore the flutters in my stomach. "What has he done today?"

"The arrogant little shit just assigned my medical appointment over my lunch hour."

I can't help but snicker. "Ah, I remember Talia saying she wanted to make sure everyone's healthy. When was your last physical?"

"Last night. Three times."

"And you're calling *Ben* arrogant?"

"Stress test, endurance, pressure check. Yep, I'm all good."

Shaking my head, I snicker, appreciating his levity. "Sorry, handsome. I won't be your excuse to get out of it."

"You're never an excuse," he says, his voice briefly lowering to a sexy, rough rumble. "I really did want to have lunch with you." Grunting his annoyance, he turns serious once more. "I swear he *tries* to get under my skin. He's like an annoying—"

"Little brother?" I interrupt.

Calder's silent for a second. "Not funny."

"I wasn't trying to be. I want you to have your family. Since your parents are gone and you don't have any siblings—yeah, I know you have Sebastian and the rest of the Blake family, but—"

"Ben's *not* family. You are."

The sudden coldness in his tone makes me feel even more desperate for my fiancé to accept his half brother into his life. "He's blood, Calder. I'm not a Blake and—"

"Let's fix that. We can go to the Justice of the Peace tomorrow. No big elaborate plans necessary. You're all I want."

But will I *be enough forever?* My heart twists as the worried thought flits through my brain for the thousandth time. "You're crazy." I laugh to smother my angst. "We're not eloping."

"You've put me off for months on setting a wedding date, Cass. I understood that you wanted to help Talia with the wedding and the birth of Joey, and then the house repairs kind of exploded on us, but that's almost done. I've been more than patient. Set a date, Raven-mine, or I swear to God one night the Pastor will just show up at our door. I'm ready to start *our* family."

It's like he just twisted a knife in my gut. I'm saved from having to respond by a deep voice in the background who Calder grumbles in response to. "I've made an executive decision. I'm exempting myself."

The baritone moves closer, Sebastian's voice coming through loud and clear. "No one's exempt, Cald. Every exam will be done today so we can get back to work. Get your ass in there."

"Fine. He's *not* touching my balls."

A snort of amusement escapes before I can stop it.

"And *you* just earned yourself a deadline, angel," Calder's voice shifts back to the phone. "I'll expect a date by this weekend."

My whole frame tenses. "It isn't as easy as snapping your fingers, Calder."

"Yes, actually it is. See you later."

He hangs up before I can counter his statement.

"That sounded intense." Beth draws my attention as she sits down at the table. "Sorry that took longer than I expected." Picking up her glass of water, she nods toward the phone I just set back on the table. "Are you and Calder doing okay?"

"We're fine." My smile feels forced as I nod. "We just have a lot going on right now."

Beth pushes her long hair over her shoulder while her gaze drops to my hand on the table. "I don't see a band next to that fabulous black diamond. While I'm glad to know that you didn't lose my invitation to your wedding, I'm surprised that you two haven't already gotten married."

I really don't want to talk about my current worries with Beth, so instead I shift the subject back to her. "You mean like you've been too busy to have lunch with me the last five times you cancelled on me?"

"Touché." Grimacing, she sets her glass down. "I deserve that."

I pick up my own glass and smile. "It's fine, Beth. I can't imagine the new CEO of a multi-million dollar business like Carver Enterprises has time for many personal lunches. Congratulations on your promotion."

Beth's lips quirk slightly as I clink my glass to hers. "I never saw myself running the family business, but with Celeste's death, then Mom passing..." She pauses and takes a deep breath. "Father took me under his wing. He's determined to teach me everything he knows in record time."

"I'm so sorry about your mom." I hold her sad gaze while we lower our glasses. "I wish you had called me. I'm always up for a talk if you don't have time for lunch."

Beth's appreciative smile doesn't light up her face like it would've in the past. The young, carefree girl I knew before Celeste's death and subsequent murder trial is gone. Beth's green eyes are less brilliant, her demeanor subdued. Careful even. She looks reserved but confident. She doesn't deserve to be lied to. I glance down at my phone. Since no other response has come through, I let myself relax. The text had to have been for someone else.

While I would love more than anything to tell Beth something that would put a happy smile on her face once more, learning the truth about Celeste wouldn't change the fact her sister is gone forever. If anything, knowing Celeste was alive, but not being able to talk to her, might destroy that layer of confidence Beth has carefully constructed around herself. I hate that it's there at all, but maybe right now...it's what she needs.

"Thank you, Cass. You don't know how much that means. And I know this might be presumptuous of me, but I...well...I really hope you think of me as a good friend. The kind who might get to help with your wedding plans?" She pauses, then quickly runs on. "After the trial and everything that happened, I don't have many friends that I can trust. And you've always been straight with me. Well, once you owned up to not being Celeste," she finishes with a quick laugh.

My stomach twists into a tighter, guilt-ridden knot.

"Thank you for offering to help, Beth. I appreciate it so much."

"Well...when is it?" she asks as she glances down at her menu.

"What?"

Her gaze snaps back to me. "Your wedding date."

"Um...well." I squirm in my seat, then look down and pretend to study my menu, hard. "We haven't really set one yet."

"Why not? The man adores you. What's stopping you?"

I glance up to see her eyebrows fully lifted. "First there was Talia's wedding, then baby Joey's arrival. We've done a lot of renovation on the house. I've got work stuff I'm trying to get going."

"Sounds like excuses to me." Lowering her menu, she frowns. "What's really going on?"

The way she's looking at me, a bit judgy edged with genuine affection...reminds me so much of my sister, my heart trips a little. It's times like this, when I'm really struggling with my own inner demons, that I miss Sophie even more than usual. Even though I had no intention of talking about it with Beth, I find myself answering. "I guess I'm waiting for the perfect time."

"Trust me..." Beth leans a bit closer. "There's *never* perfect timing. Something will always come up. If you love him, set a date...so then I can be a part of it."

And just like something Sophie would've said, Beth gives a matter-of-fact, self-indulgent response. I laugh and squeeze her hand on the table. "I promise to let you know."

Beth quickly turns her hand over in mine and folds them together. Suddenly releasing me, she shakes her head, her gaze misty. "I'm sorry, Cass. For a second I felt like I was talking to Celeste...well, the way she was when we were younger."

I recapture her hand and turn ours over so my raven tattoo is face up. I'm proud that as stressed as I am, my wrist hasn't itched. Knowing the symbol I had tattooed over my old cutting scars and the word "Never" along my forearm to remind me of my promise to my sister to "never give up on myself" helps, and so does Beth's sweet smile. "You reminded me of my sister just now too."

A couple tears trail her cheeks. "I think they'd be happy we have each other, don't you?"

Just as I nod, my phone buzzes with a new text.

You know who this is.

CHAPTER TWO

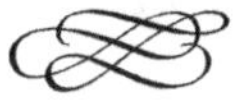

CALDER

"I'm done," I grunt, sliding my arm back into my light-blue dress shirt. I'm annoyed as hell that Bash is making me do this, but the fact Cass vaguely mentioned some business thing she has today, which I had no clue about, only to brush off my suggestion of eloping after she'd put off setting a wedding date for months… Well, I'm more than on edge.

Ben scans the tablet in his hand and taps on the screen, his brown eyes snapping back to me. "Not so fast. You need to fill out the entire form, including the medical history section. No food or coffee yet, right? I'll also need to get a vial of your blood."

I tug the shirt back over my shoulder and glance down past the Celtic Solus tattoo on my torso to the scar on my hip just above my dress pants' waistline. "Since you patched me up after your psychotic father shot me, you're familiar with this wound, Hemming. There's nothing else to discuss. I'm healthy. End of story."

He stiffens at my dig. I stare at him, daring him to voice the thought that's stamped on his face: *He's* your *father too.* "That's *Doctor* Hemming. A complete medical history is important, Calder."

"You're not my doctor." We glare at each other, neither willing to back off. He has some underlying agenda and I'm not playing into his bullshit.

"I am today."

"I don't have to disclose anything to you," I say, glancing down to focus on buttoning my shirt cuff so I don't punch that smug smirk. I ignore the twinge in my shoulder where a shrapnel fragment still annoys me every so often. My fingers fumble as the pain flares, so I flex my fingers before finally pushing the button through.

"How's your grip?" Ben asks.

His tone might be matter-of-fact, but I suddenly curl my hand into a threatening fist and narrow my gaze. "You tell me."

He snorts. "If you want to work in the field with the rest of the BLACK Security team, your full medical history, including parents, siblings, etc...it all needs to be documented, Calder."

"Fuck this." Walking out of his office, I head straight for my own and slam the door behind me.

A few minutes later, my door opens. I don't look up from the new client field report I'm reading. When someone takes a seat in front of my desk, I snap, "The door is closed for a reason."

"I see your morning is going well."

I meet my cousin's steady blue gaze as he sets a mug of coffee on my desk before taking a sip from his own mug. Not once—since I've come to work here—has he brought me coffee. I don't trust it.

"Either he goes or I do," I say. When he chuckles into his mug, my gaze narrows. "You don't think I'm serious?"

Dark eyebrows elevate. "Oh, I think you're serious as hell, but before you go off half-cocked, I'd like to hear your reasoning. Sure would hate to lose a good partner."

"You're choosing him over me?" I scowl. "What the fuck, Bash?"

"You're the one taking sides, Cald. BLACK Security is a team. And a team only works well together if there's trust. What has your brother done now?"

"Stop calling him my goddamn brother." I lift the mug so I don't pound a hole in my desk. When Bash doesn't reply, but instead takes his time with another sip of coffee, I do the same, waiting him out.

"It's a simple statement of fact."

"*You* grew up with me. That's a brother."

His blue gaze suddenly sharpens. "Then start talking."

"He insisted on my full medical history," I grit out.

"We all provided it." He shrugs. "Fill out the form, Calder. It's no big deal."

My fingers tighten on the mug. "You're missing the point. I have no fucking clue what my real medical history is, certainly not on my father's side."

"I see." Bash settles deeper in the chair. "Ben wouldn't be doing his job thoroughly if he didn't ask you to fill out that information."

I shoot him an "are you fucking kidding me?" look. "He knows I can't fill out that form without asking him for *our* father's medical history," I say, barely keeping my tone civil. "It's like he's rubbing the fact that sick fuck forced himself on my mother in my face. As far as I'm concerned, I buried my only father."

Bash rests his mug on my desk, then sets his elbows on his knees, leaning forward. "I know that this is like scraping open a raw wound for you, but documenting your medical history doesn't erase your personal one, Calder. Jack will always be your father. Those memories will never go away, but the fact remains that Phillip Hemming unfortunately was the sperm donor. I'm just glad he's already in jail so you can't commit murder. Let Ben be a great source of information. That way you won't have to ask the man directly."

"Why the hell would I ever want to know anything about him?"

Bash shakes his head. "I hope you'll never need to, but information is important. Knowing if something might be coming down the line for you, health-wise, is just strategically smart, Cald."

Picking up his mug, my cousin stands and turns for the door. With his hand on the knob, he looks back at me. "While you're sitting here stewing in anger and resentment, consider the fact that the only time I've seen you speak at any length to Ben is when he was annoying the piss out of you. You could be right that he had an ulterior motive with this medical history bit, but I think you're way off about the reason behind it.

"That guy's father and brother are rotting in prison for their part in the shit that went down with the Carver family. Now that Ben has cut himself off from half his family, he's probably trying to make sense of his life too. Dial back the asshole, Cald. Be the guy who spun out a tire wheel. Like you, Ben didn't ask for any of this."

As Bash starts to walk out, I grumble, "Minus the asshole comment, the rest of that sounded suspiciously like Talia."

He doesn't even look back as he snaps, "Orphan asshole."

I stare at the open doorway and despite my mood, I bark out a laugh. I haven't thought about that moment in years...

Holding my motorcycle helmet under my arm, I called out as I started toward the garage. "Be back at dinnertime."

"Hold up," Dad said from the living room where he and Sebastian were watching a golf tournament. Well, they were both watching, but Sebastian was listening to music on his headphones. I sighed my annoyance and waited for him to come into the foyer where he spoke in a low tone. "You should take Bash with you."

This had been going on since the beginning of the summer four weeks ago. I set my jaw. "Stop insisting I take him with me whenever I make plans with friends, Dad. He has his own friends. If he's bored, he can go running, play basketball, or something."

"He left his friends behind when he moved. He'll be starting over at your school in less than a month. And, yes, he'll probably play a sport and make friends that way, but until then, help him transition. He just lost his mom, Calder. Things haven't gone well at his dad and Isabel's house. He's family. Blakes support each other."

It was on the tip of my tongue to correct him that Sebastian was technically half-family, but that would've earned me a hard stare and probably a week of grounding. Why did my father seem to care so much about Sebastian's feelings? What about my feelings? I didn't get any say-so in the guy coming to live with us. It didn't help that Sebastian and my father seemed to get along so well, while lately it felt like Dad and I were always butting heads. This was bullshit. "I only have one bike and so does Liam, so—"

"Then let Sebastian ride with you."

With my father's annoying insistence that I include my cousin in my social life, all he'd managed to do was make Sebastian a thorn in my side. Ever since Uncle Adam came to our house with this kid sporting one brown eye and one blue, my life had sucked. I remembered how pissed Sebastian looked while his father spoke to mine in his office. Then my uncle walked out of my dad's office, retrieved a couple suitcases from his car, and his illegitimate son had lived with us since.

The last thing I wanted to do during my senior year of high school was babysit my "new" cousin. Yet so far, that's how my summer was shaping up. Needless to say, I hadn't made an effort to get to know Sebastian. As far as I was concerned, he was just a constant pain in my ass.

"Are you going to build those planter boxes, Jack?" Sebastian called from the couch as he tugged his headphones down to his neck. "I'll be happy to help."

"Are you sure?" My dad was already rubbing his hands together, his gaze lighting with excitement.

Sebastian lifted the remote and turned the TV off. "If we start now, we can probably get them built and set up today."

"At least then we can save some plants from those

damn rabbits. Just let me change clothes." Turning to me, Dad said, "Be home before six, Calder."

My gaze snapped between the two of them. Before I moved up to high school and started driving, I would've loved to work on a project like that with my dad. I should be relieved that he wasn't insisting I stay and help. Instead, I was slightly irritated. I started to say something, but the house phone rang. I knew it was Liam calling to tell me to hurry up and meet him at the gate at the entrance to our property.

"Okay, then. I guess I'll see you guys later."

"See ya," my father called out absently as he jogged up the stairs to change clothes.

I ENDED *up cutting my day short with Liam. Partially because I'd grown tired of just riding around, but also because I was honest enough with myself to admit I was jealous of Sebastian spending so much time with my father. As far as I knew, he'd never had a cross word with my dad. And to hear my father talk about him...well, Sebastian was a freaking angel.*

My cousin's t-shirt was coated with sweat and dirt stains as he pushes a wheelbarrow full of dirt from the side of the house to the front. Saw dust and dirt clods coat the front drive where they'd built the planters and had already started to fill them. Once they were fully done, they'd be set next to the columns on either side of the front porch. "Where's Dad?" I asked after I cut the engine and lifted my helmet off.

Sebastian pulled off his work gloves and glanced up at the darkening sky. "He went to the store for some plants and topsoil."

When I didn't say anything else, he turned back around and slid the gloves back on.

The planters' nice clean lines looked great, which only annoyed me more, so I narrowed my gaze on his broad back and folded my arm around the helmet. "You know he's not your father, right? He will never *be your dad."*

"I have a father," Sebastian said, his dual-colored gaze swinging sharply my way. "As shitty as he is...he's still mine. I'm not trying to steal yours, Calder."

I stiffened and glanced away to secure my helmet to the back of my bike. "I didn't say you were trying to steal—"

"From the moment I got here, you've been an asshole."

"Yeah, well..." I scowled and settled back into my seat. Arms folded and feet firmly planted to keep the bike balanced, I figured I should just be honest with the guy. "I don't like being forced to—"

"Look, I've got one more year and I'm out of here. You'll never have to see me again. I'm not trying to be anyone's son. *I'm just glad to be living in a place where people aren't constantly stabbing me in the back and*

judging me for having the fucking nerve to be born." He paused and narrowed his gaze, his jaw hardening. "Unless that's about to change."

I started to speak when a car comes up the long drive, drawing our attention. Gavin pulled in front of us in his silver Beamer, then he and Damien stepped out and leaned on each of their doors.

"Well, well...look at that, Damien," Gavin drawled, glancing at his younger brother across the top of his car. "I'm glad to see Uncle Jack has the orphan *doing work that fits his background."*

Damien laughs. "I wonder if he serves them food too? You know, following in the footsteps of his mother?"

At the same time Sebastian fists the shovel handle in a death grip, my whole body tenses. Orphan? Just because Gavin and Damien hate that their dad fathered another son not long before he married their mom doesn't give them a right to be total asswipes.

"Stop being dicks and grow the fuck up," I snapped. Quickly starting my engine, I spun my bike around to put it between the guys and said to Sebastian in an even tone, "It's going to rain soon. I'll put this away and help."

When Sebastian's gaze met mine, I flashed an evil grin and squealed my tire, sending dirt clods and saw dust scattering like buckshot all over my cousin's car as I took off for the garage on the side of the house.

Parking quickly, I hopped off my bike and just as I

walked out of the garage, I froze at the sight of Sebastian aiming a handgun toward my cousins' car while they drove away toward our gated entrance.

As I bolted toward him, he popped off a few rounds, hitting both back tires, then set the gun down and started shoveling as if nothing had happened.

It was my dad's pellet gun. *Snorting my relief, I slowed my frantic pace and reached him as he dumped a new shovel of dirt into the planter.*

"Not such an angel after all, are you?" I say, glancing at the gun tucked in its holder on the ground near the wheelbarrow.

"Never claimed to be." Sebastian didn't say anything else as he held out the other shovel.

"We orphans *need to stick together. Welcome to the Blake family," I said, grinning as I took it from him. "Want to place a bet how long their tires will take to deflate?"*

As the memory fades, I rub my jaw and grunt at the irony of that day, considering that I never had any Blake blood running through my veins. *Could Bash be right?* Am I blowing this way out of proportion and Ben wasn't rubbing my bastard existence in my face, but instead trying to get my attention?

I pick up my mug and lean back in my chair, feeling like an ass for not giving that option a thought. Rolling my head from one shoulder to the other, I start to reach for the phone to call Ben, when he walks into my office, tablet in hand.

"Are you done pitching a fit? 'Cause we really need to get back to business. I have a schedule to keep," he says in a matter-of-fact tone. Without a beat, he sits down and glances at the screen, scrolling through it. "Let's start from the top. I noticed that you didn't check your marital status. Has Cass finally set a date?" Glancing up, his lips quirk. "She's not getting cold feet, is she?"

"Out!" I set my mug down so hard the coffee sloshes over my hand. I'm so pissed, the heat doesn't even register.

"Whoa, calm down. I was just joking, bro." Shaking his head, Ben looks back at the screen. "Okay, back to this... you also didn't list your blood type. If you don't remember, it should be on your dog tags. If you end up marrying Cass, and she's negative and you're positi—"

If I marry her? I haven't forgotten the asshole telling me he'd fight me for Cass if I didn't do right by her last year. And now he's trying to cast doubt about our future together? "Get. The. Fuck, *Out*," I growl.

Ben's brows pull together, his gaze snapping to mine. "Are you serious?"

When he doesn't move, I quickly stand and lean across the desk, my stance full of lethal intent. "You won't like my idea of putting you out myself."

CHAPTER THREE

CASS

"I need you to drill deeper into his financials, Elijah." Talia opens a folder on her desk while holding her phone to her ear. She nods at me as I walk into her office, but keeps talking. "Right. Pull everything you can find so I can go over them. Look for offshore accounts, shell companies, also check recent real estate sales. I've just finished compiling the evidence to prove his wife's death wasn't an accident, but the case will be stronger for the police if we can find the person responsible. The husband's too smart to have done it himself. He paid for that hit. We need to see that money going out and trace it. I want Celia to be able to bury her mother in peace."

While Talia gives Elijah more detailed instructions, I watch her face bloom with desire for justice. I've seen her in action dozens of times across the years and it never gets old. She's truly doing what she was born to do, which makes me smile at the memory of how Talia and I became best friends.

I rolled my eyes at Jodi and Samantha sitting in the corner booth, soaking up the free drinks the four guys have been ordering for them the past two hours. The joke's on the guys, because soon the girls' boyfriends would show up, along with their fraternity brothers, and boot the guys the hell out of that booth.

I came with the girls, but when I saw what they were up to, I moved over to the bar to order my own drink. The first time, it was an adrenaline rush watching their men get all alpha and rush in to bounce the interlopers on their asses, but then, the next time it happened, I realized it was all a well planned scam. The girls got free drinks and the boyfriends not only saved money, but it gave them an excuse to get into a brawl if the guys didn't back off their girls. I sure as hell didn't want to be a part of it.

After I flashed my fake ID to the bartender and he set my mojito on the wood bar top, an adorable blond guy with longish surfer hair sat on the stool next to me. "Whatcha drinking, good looking?"

I smirked at his hair brushing his collar, thinking that it was an interesting contrast to his preppy-boy clothes, and took a sip of my drink. "Mojito." I nodded to his beer. "Imported or domestic?"

"Whatever's the special." He took several swallows of his beer, his blue eyes never leaving mine. "I find it hard to believe you're here alone. Where's your posse?"

Enjoying his undivided attention, I glanced back at the girls and shook my head. Another round of beers, girls? Really? *"They're back there, being a couple of freeloaders with indiscriminate palates."*

He laughed and nodded to my drink. "I take it mojitos taste much better than free beer?"

"Well, the free part is always nice, but yep." Just as I lifted my glass to my lips, someone behind me tapped my shoulder.

"Excuse me. What is that drink called?"

I turned, and the moment I saw the redhead and how her attention wasn't on my drink but on the guy next to me, I narrowed my gaze. No way are you horning in on this, girlie! *"It's a mojito," I said in a tone meant to shut her down, then immediately put my back to her.*

She tapped my shoulder again. "How much was it?"

"Less than ten," I said, then glanced at the bartender as he approached. "Ask him, sheesh."

"Is that your black sports car parked right out front?" she said to the guy beside me, completely missing all my cues for her to leave us alone. He looked as annoyed as I felt, but still nodded. "Oh, I only ask because I saw some guys leaning on it. I was surprised that didn't set your alarm off."

"It should have." He scowled and jerked his gaze to the door. "I'll be right back."

The moment he moved away, I set my drink down and rounded on her. "Look, Red Riding Hood, I've tried to be nice, but you need to walk away and stop trying to steal this guy's attention."

Instead of taking my advice, she dipped her pinky into my drink, then flipped her wet finger upright, her lips tilted in a "total attitude" smirk.

"Awww, all you've got is that little feather? Here's the whole bird," I said and flipped her off. "Go away!"

Rolling her eyes, she opened her whole hand and spoke in a low, urgent tone, "Look at my nail polish. The color changes when it comes into contact with known drugs. He spiked your drink when you looked away."

I stared at the black polish on her pinky compared to her hot pink nails and my face grew hot with my near miss. Before I could thank her, she quickly dropped her hand and turned away just as the surfer guy walked up to my side once more. "Guess they're gone now," he said, a charming smile on his face. "Want to go sit alone in a booth?"

Ticked at what he'd almost done to me, I picked up my drink, intending to dump it on his head, but then I saw Jodi and Samantha's boyfriends and their buddies just outside the bar through the picture window and I set my drink back down. Forcing a broad smile, I said, "Sure, I can hang, but..." I paused and tilted my chin the redhead's way.

"She's new here, so I told her I'd introduce her to some of my friends. Be right back."

"Come on" I grabbed the girl's hand and pulled her with me to the front of the bar and out the door. Once I spotted the ringleader of the fraternity crew, I tapped his thick shoulder. "Hey, Bradly." As soon as he swiveled his dark head my way, I thumbed back toward the bar. "See the surfer looking guy in the teal polo shirt sitting at the bar? I saw him slip a drug into that mojito on the bar top, and well, you know how much Jodi likes mojitos. Might want to go take care of that."

When he stormed into the bar, his guys following behind, ready to rumble, the redhead watched them with rapt anticipation. "I noticed that guy trolling a couple weeks ago. Every time I saw him here, I spilled drinks, horned in, and basically did everything I could think of to redirect unsuspecting girls. Why should they believe me? Hence, the polish. So far I haven't seen him working with anyone else, but you were the last straw. I planned to report him tonight..." She paused as Bradly grabbed the jerk by the shirt collar before he could walk out, and called to the bartender, who scowled, then picked up his phone. "But this scenario works for me."

"Thanks for looking out for me. I'm Cass. So what's your name, my new best friend for life?" Smiling, I held out my pinky.

"I'm Talia." She grinned and hooked her black pinky nail with mine. "And you're welcome."

"Please tell me you're a student here too?" I asked. When she nodded, I released her and bumped shoulders. "Want to walk back with me?"

"Sounds good to me," she said and we fell in step together.

I was silent for a bit. She would never know how much I would always freaking love her for what she did. "You know..." I give her the side eye. "You're pretty observant, Talia. With your skills, you should consider taking a class to hone that talent. Maybe something related to investigative work?"

She smiles "I've been thinking about something along those lines. I'm not sure what just yet."

"Oooh, I know. Have you looked into the school paper? They're always writing about some injustice or another. Might be a good fit for you."

Talia looked intrigued as she walked. "Thanks for the suggestion, Cass. I'll have to check it out."

"Why are you grinning like crazy?" Talia's amused question pulls me back to the present.

"Just thinking about how I was instrumental in the beginning of your badass investigative career." I smirk and step forward as she sets her phone down.

She chuckles. "Oh, you mean the day you gave me the finger?"

"The one and only. Here are the photos you asked for." I set the thumb drive on her desk and try to ignore the nervous jump in my heart rate.

"Ha, that wasn't the *only* time." She reminds me as she plugs the drive into her laptop. "You know you could've emailed them and saved yourself a trip."

"I just like your cute face." I give her a *mwah* air kiss, then gesture to the computer. "Have a look. I know you thought it was a couple days' job, but taking a week to study the place paid off."

While Talia tucks her long auburn hair behind her ear and slides the drive into her laptop, I quickly walk around her desk. "Oh, how'd Calder's medical exam go?"

Talia purses her lips. "Let's just say Calder won't be adding Ben as his own personal doctor any time soon."

"Those two need to be locked in a room together." Sighing my disappointment, I shake my head. "Then they'd be forced to talk and would eventually work out their differences."

Her green gaze flicks to me as she opens the images folder on her computer. "Whether intentional or not, Ben has a special knack for pushing Calder's buttons. At this point, maybe a good brawl would rectify their issues."

For Talia to suggest they duke it out isn't a good sign. "I think it's hard for Calder to separate Ben from his last name...and his connection to Phillip."

"I understand and empathize." Talia sighs and shakes

her head. "But something's going to have to give. Trust is key for the whole team to work."

"I'll try to talk to him."

Smiling her appreciation, she taps on the first image I'd highlighted for her.

"I just downloaded all the photos from this week, but sorted by the ones I thought mattered," I say as she scrolls over to the next one. "As you can see, there are three ways people can leave that building. Four if you count those guys hopping from the adjacent building's roof to smoke on the rooftop."

She raises an eyebrow and looks at me. "Good catch on the rooftop, Cass. Another access point we'll need to cover for this event."

"Who's the client, anyway?" My nerves wind tighter as I take my time getting to the question I need to ask.

"A high-profile judge. His daughter's wedding reception will be held here."

"Ah, well then. You should be good to go."

Talia nods and emails the file to Sebastian. "I've got another job coming up in two weeks if you want it."

"Hopefully I'll be able to fit it in. I'll let you know this weekend." Shifting from one foot to the other in my heeled sandals, I rub my sweaty palms down the front of my royal-blue sundress. "Speaking of jobs, I know you normally send out freelance payments mid-month, but would it be possible to get mine today?"

Talia's brows pull together. "Of course, Cass. Is everything all right?"

"Yeah." I swallow to keep my voice steady and confident. I love my best friend, but I hate depending on someone else for my livelihood. "The last advance I got should help me ride things through until I get this other book turned into my editor."

She stands and clasps my hand, tugging me to fully face her. "If you're looking for steady work, I'm sure we can find a role in BLACK Security for you. I'm sorry if I haven't asked before now, but I didn't think you were interested in working here on a permanent basis."

"No, that's not it." I fold my other hand over hers and squeeze. "I'm working on getting my own space. You know how much they scrutinize your income history and how mine has been a bit up and down lately. Having more in the bank should help with their requirements, especially since I've worked with this agent before. Judith Anders is the one who helped me get our last apartment."

"Cass!" Talia's green eyes widen. "Why didn't you tell me? If space is what you need, I'm sure we can find room for you to do your work here." Nodding, she mumbles, "Elijah's got that second office and we could do a bit of renovation and—"

"No, Talia." I quickly cut her off, then smile to soften my sudden strident tone. "Thank you, but I'm good. Do you remember how I needed to get out of our apartment sometimes to think and come up with new ideas for shoots? It's like that. For what I have in mind...I'll need a studio and space to be creative."

"I can't believe Calder's family estate doesn't have enough room to accommodate you."

"It's not that. I need something in the city. Closer to everything."

"Ah, I see. Are you going back to full time photography?" Her excited gaze quickly drops to the tattoo on my left wrist, then shifts back to my face. "Wait? Are you bringing Raven back?" Pausing, she suddenly frowns. "Your magazine photography was a lot of travel, Cass. If Calder's anything like Sebastian, he would hate if you traveled all the time. And speaking selfishly...so would I. I've loved having my best friend around."

"Calm down, Miss Deductive Reasoning." I shake my head. "I'm not quite sure how this business model will look just yet, but yes, it'll involve photography and I'll be working with clients. I just need to figure out the right set-up that'll give me sustained business, but hopefully won't require the kind of travel I had to do in the past."

"I'm so excited for you, Cass. And of course...I'll be happy to loan you the money to get set up if you need it."

"Thanks for offering, but once I get paid, I've got this."

Talia's expression softens. "If you say so. I'll put your payment in before you leave, but...are you sure you'll be okay? I mean, how's the timing of getting a new business off the ground going to work with doing side jobs for us? And what about your wedding? Speaking of which, you really need to set a date. If you need me to step in and coordinate things like you did for me, I'll be happy to—"

"The date's coming," I say quickly. Talia's peppering me with so many questions, I blink to remain calm, but my chest constricts with anxiety. When my wrist begins to itch uncontrollably, I press my arm against my thigh and briefly close my eyes, exhaling a calm breath. "It'll all be fine. Don't worry."

Soft hands clasp my cheeks and she forces me to look at her. "No, you're not. What's going on?"

Those stupid texts are niggling in the back of my mind, but I don't want to think about them on top of everything else going on; they could still be from someone just messing around. So instead I tell her what's bothering me the most. "With Calder still pushing Ben away...what if...I'm not enough family for him, Talia?"

Her gaze searches mine. "Of course you're enough, silly. The way he looks at you...you're everything to Calder."

"But will I be in five years? What about ten years down the road? I told you we haven't used birth control in months. Will he hate that he married someone who can't give him children?"

Talia tugs me into a tight hug. "He's not marrying you for the potential baby factory you might be. He's marrying *you.*" Pulling back, she brushes my hair away from my face as I sniff back the mist suddenly blurring my vision. "You don't even know if there's an issue medically. There could be another explanation—"

"I had to know, so I went to my doctor." I sigh heavily, my voice shaking. "He said my uterus is tilted, which could make it harder to conceive. And since my mom started menopause earlier than the average woman, he took some blood to check my AMH level. The anti-mullerian hormone is an indicator of the health and quality of my eggs. Anyway, if the number is low, then I could have issues conceiving. I've been on edge ever since I discovered I might truly have an issue. I'm waiting to get the results back."

"He said *could*, Cass. Not impossible." Lowering her hands to my shoulders, she massages my tense muscles. "I know you're nervous about the results, but if you end up having to do treatments, you do. None of that will change how much Calder loves you."

I rest my cheek on her hand on my shoulder, giving a lopsided smile. She sounds so confident, I half believe her. "I know you're right." *I just wish I could see into the future and know he won't resent me one day.*

Turning her hand to cup my face, she returns my smile. "Of course I'm right."

I can tell by her expression that she's still concerned about me, so I straighten and force a wide smile. "I'll be fine, Talia. Truly. Don't worry. In the meantime, I have a business to work on. Do you want to come see the space with me?"

"I would love to come see it with you. When are you going?"

I glance at my watch. "My appointment with the agent is at two-thirty."

Talia's excited expression falls. "Ugh, I'm sorry, Cass. I thought it might be much later today. Sebastian and I are heading out to interview the lady who will be taking over Teresa's housekeeping duties just as soon as he gets a conference call kicked off and handed over to Calder."

"Wait? Where is Teresa going? She's been with Sebastian forever, right?"

Talia smiles. "When she found out we were interviewing potential nannies, she insisted she wanted the role. She adores our little girl so much and Joey really responds to her. You'd think that would make the decision an easy one. I consider myself a calm mother who's not afraid to bring out the tiger claws when necessary, but Sebastian makes me look like a pussycat."

When I start to laugh, she snorts. "Seriously, Cass... you wouldn't believe how he drilled her, from how she planned to care for and stimulate our child, to safety protocols for whenever she takes her out for a stroll or to the park. Most people would've cracked under that kind of pressure, but Teresa's one tough cookie."

"It sounds like she's the clear winner, right? Only the best for my goddaughter," I say, wagging my finger at her.

Talia smiles and nods. "But that means we have to hire someone to help with some of her old duties, and after watching Sebastian before..." She sighs. "I'm only going today so he doesn't break the poor woman, who happens to be Teresa's younger sister."

"Surely Teresa would've prepared her?" I've seen firsthand how intense Sebastian can be when it comes to protecting his family. And I'm sure he's not that much different with business interests. "I'll just count myself lucky that he's not the one I report to for these BLACK Security freelance jobs."

"Ha, I'm pretty sure you'd give Sebastian hell if he tried that with you, but yeah, I just think it'll be better if I'm there." Talia turns to straighten the papers and folders on her desk into a neat stack, then closes her laptop. Turning back to me, she pouts her disappointment. "So long story short...I'm really sorry I won't be able to go look at that space with you."

"What space?"

My heart leaps at the familiar voice. I quickly turn to see Calder in the doorway connecting Talia's office to Sebastian's. "Oh, hey. How'd your appointment go?" I ask in hopes that Talia was exaggerating. When he scowls and curls his hand into a fist by his side, I cut a look Talia's way. She wasn't.

"What space, Cass?"

"Oh, it's just for a project I'm working on." I give Talia a quick hug, then walk around her desk to pick up my purse. Sliding the strap onto my shoulder, I check my watch, then blow him a kiss as I stride toward the doorway. "Sorry, I've got to run if I want to be there on time."

Before he can ask me anything else, I walk out of Talia's office at a fast pace, intending to quickly make my way to the main entrance.

Just as I start to pass Sebastian's office, I slam into a tall wall of muscle encased in a custom suit. Warm hands fold over my bare arms, locking me in place. "*Where* are you going, Raven-mine?"

I shift my gaze upward, past his defined jawline to his penetrating green eyes staring at me with a mixture of irritation and concern. "I told you. To look at a space."

"Why didn't you mention this project before now?" His light-brown brows pull together. "Is this a new freelance gig you're renting temporary space for?"

The feel of his thumbs sliding along my skin sets off a round of chill bumps, making my pulse race. I love this man so much, my heart twists just looking at his handsome face. Even when he's scowling at me, I want to reach up and run my fingers through his thick short hair, to pull him close and press my lips to his sexy mouth, to feel his teeth on my skin.

But I tamp down the urge, because that'll just give

him more time to try to drill me for details. I know he'll want to get involved. The protective alpha male in him wouldn't have it any other way. Of course he would want to make it easier. If only it were that easy for him to fix me too. I have to—I *need*—to do this for myself.

With emotions surging, I swallow so my voice doesn't crack. "No, it's just a personal project I want to do, Calder." Rising up on my toes, I quickly kiss his jaw and inhale his wonderful aftershave. "I really do need to go though. I'll see you tonight."

I move around him and start to walk away, but he clasps my hand. "Wait, I'll take you—"

"The conference call is starting in three minutes," Sebastian calls from inside his office.

Leaning into the doorway, Calder says, "Take this one. I have something I need to do."

"You brought us this client, Cald. You need to be on the call. Talia and I will be leaving for our appointment after the call starts."

"Is this that really big contract you just landed?" I tug free of Calder's hold and *shoo* him on. "Take the call! That's important. I've got to go or I'll be late."

"I can drop you off if you need a ride." Ben pauses beside us in the hallway, keys in hand. "I'm going to 20th. Where are you headed?"

When Calder cuts a sharp look his way, I smile at Ben to soften the blow. "That's nice of you to offer,

Ben, but I'm good. I'm heading to look at a place in Midtown and will just take the train, since the listing is close to the station." I look at my watch and move away from them, heading toward the entrance. "I really do need to go." Glancing back at Calder, I wave and keep my tone light. "I hope your call goes well. Wish me luck."

"I'll meet you there."

The insistent Blake expression on his face makes me glad he's stuck in the office. He would totally take over and that's the last thing I want right now. I need to win at *something*. "Don't worry. I've got this."

"Wait up, Cass. We can walk out together," Ben says, rushing to catch up.

"Where are you going?" Calder drills after him. "Don't you have people to check?"

"My most difficult patient bailed, so I'm done for the day." Ben turns once he reaches the door to meet Calder's hard gaze across the open cubical space. "I'll be at the shooting range."

"Moving targets are much harder." Calder frowns, folding his arms.

"They also don't bleed. 'Do No Harm' and all that," Ben lobs back as he pulls the door open for me.

Hating the tension between the men, I say, "See you tonight," to my fiancé in a cheery tone before I follow Ben out.

"So is this a work thing?" Ben asks while we walk toward the elevator.

"Yep, a new project."

Talia's bodyguard walks off the elevator. Den's massive six-five height might intimidate, but it's his panther-like confidence that always draws my appreciation. "Cass, Ben," he says smoothly, nodding to us. "Have a good afternoon."

"You too," I say as he heads for the office. "Den really does have a nice accent, doesn't he?" I mumble half to myself.

"Do *all* women love a British accent?" Ben snorts, amused.

"Yep, it's like a mini ear massage, all pleasant and *smoooooth*," I say, grinning as Ben pushes the button.

Once the elevator doors close and we start to move down, he looks at me. "If your project's anything like your New York City book, I'm sure it'll do very well."

"You've seen my book?" It feels good to hear that someone other than my editor, parents, Calder, and Talia like my book, so I grin like crazy.

"I *bought* your book. It's awesome, Cass. You really have an eye for amazing photography. Your skills are totally wasted taking surveillance pictures for the company. As your ex-fiancé, I think I have a right to give my opinion."

My lips twitch in amusement, then settle into a smile.

During my brief time as Celeste, a surprise engagement was announced, cementing a merger between the Hemming and Carver families. Ben became my fiancé. Well, technically Celeste's fiancé. By the time Ben discovered that I wasn't actually Celeste, he and I had become friends. We never got around to discussing details about my career as a photographer. What would he think if I told him my work has been in magazines for years?

I released my New York City book under my real name. I didn't let my publisher connect it to the well-known photographer in the fashion world, Raven. Even on my website bio, my face was purposefully obscured. I enjoyed the fact that Raven worked in the background and only my model clients, their book agencies and the magazines knew the face behind the camera.

I wanted my new work to stand on its own, not be a fraction of a much bigger publication. Then again, my recent book didn't come anywhere close to the sales all those very established high-end magazines have. Getting published was a humbling experience after Raven's meteoric rise in the high-fashion photography world. I'll find a way to rebuild my brand again. I'll Phoenix my way through if necessary.

"Just don't mention that ex-fiancée joke in front of Calder," I say, laughing as we reach the main floor lobby. "I'm so glad you loved the book, Ben. And yes, to answer your question, this is a serious photography venture, not a freelance gig."

Once we're outside on the sidewalk, he nods his approval and slides his hands into his slacks pockets. "Good for you. And since my ornery brother didn't manage to say it, I'll pass along the well wishes. Best of luck today."

I smile my thanks and stare after him while he heads for his car. He might not be as tall or as openly aggressive as Calder can be, but Ben's just as stubborn as his brother in his own way. His mettle simmers just under the surface. Both men have good hearts. I know their horrible father is a wedge between them. Phillip Hemming not only destroyed Celeste's life, but his sons' too with his despicable actions. I just wish Calder would allow himself to see Ben as his family, instead of as a constant reminder of a past he wished didn't exist.

I start to turn toward the station, when I get a text from Judith.

Will be fifteen minutes late. The landlord said he'd let you in and I'll meet you there. FYI, I couldn't get in touch with your father. That could be a problem.

CHAPTER FOUR

CASS

The sun feels hot on my skin as I come up from the station. On the ride over, each rhythmic bump of the wheels on the track wound my nerves tighter and tighter. I'd dialed my dad's cell number without thinking, then quickly hung up once I remembered my parents are enjoying an unplugged vacation. I'm thrilled that my father finally took some time off. He's never taken more than a long weekend away from work while I was growing up, but if the agent will need more details from him, the timing of his absence will suck.

I'm probably worrying unnecessarily. I've worked with Judith before with no issue. And that was while I was a senior in college with no work history.

I let out my breath slowly, seeking a Zen mindset as I head up the street.

As the apartment building comes into view, I slow my steps and take in the area now that I have a bit more time. Even in a less busy neighborhood, people walk briskly—as New Yorkers do. The area is just outside of Manhattan, which makes me happy that it's close enough without the astronomical rent I'd pay just a couple streets over. According to the details online, this building only has a few apartments in it, and the one that's available, 2B, has more space than the others.

Which makes me wonder why the rent is so reasonable. Is there some undesirable element in this neighborhood I'm unaware of? I scan the street ahead of me. Other than people walking, I see a couple of kids goofing off. Just as I turn to look behind me, I catch someone moving quickly into the alley between this building and the next.

I narrow my gaze and watch the corner, waiting. I'm pretty sure I saw that there's no exit between the two buildings when I passed it, so whoever went in...must eventually come out. A couple minutes pass and I glance at my phone at Judith's new text.

Stuck in traffic. See you in five.

An older lady passes me and starts up the steps to the building, lugging a two-wheeled cart behind her.

"Here, let me help you." I quickly lift the cart for her, then follow her inside.

"Thank you," she mumbles without even looking my

way, then pulls her cart through the entryway and down a hall toward the elevator.

I start to follow when my gaze snags on the door in front of me: 2B.

Did I somehow miss a floor while walking inside? I frown at the door and start to touch the number, but the latch gives and the door opens.

Maybe the landlord unlocked it for us? I hesitate for a second, then I walk in and push the door almost closed. I inhale the fresh coat of paint on the stark white walls, and the scent of floor cleaner too. I walk quietly across the wood floor, past the two windows, then turn toward the room, trying to picture where I would set my desk up. Shelves would line the walls behind it to hold all my camera equipment and special lighting. I'll have to invest in a few photo backdrops. I'm thankful I have plenty of landscape imagery I could use for some fun versions too.

The kitchen is cute and small, but will do.

Stepping into the short hallway on the other side of the room, I open one door. Small closet. The door next to it, yep, a tiny bathroom. I turn and open the door on the opposite side of the hall and smile. Ah, the bedroom's actually nice-sized. I expected smaller for the price. Noise from outside floats my way and once I step into the bedroom, I realize the window has been left cracked to air out the paint fumes.

The buzz of a new text comes through. Must be Judith waiting outside.

I won't let you ignore me.

Blood rushes in my ears and my heart thumps against my chest. *Is this Celeste playing some kind of sick game?* Ugh, I wish I could block a blocked number. I quickly tap out a response.

Whoever this is, STOP texting me.

Right after I hit send, a slamming sound jerks my heart into overdrive. Clutching my phone to my chest, I quietly step to the doorway and peer around the bedroom door. The apartment door is completely closed now. *Did someone follow me in here? Could the person be lurking just out of my line of sight?*

Sweat coats my palms and my breathing ramps. I take a deep breath and bolt for the apartment door as fast as I can. Jerking it open, I run right into Calder.

"Where's the fire?" he grunts, grabbing hold of me. He looks at me and his hold tightens, all amusement gone. "What's wrong?"

I glance back briefly into the empty apartment, then take a breath to calm my overactive imagination. Returning my gaze to his concerned one, I shrug. "Nothing. I realized I probably wasn't supposed to enter by myself."

His brows pull together in doubt, then he glances over

my shoulder into the apartment, his expression turning hard. "You said 'space for a project.'"

"Yep, it's exactly what I was looking for." I turn and gesture to the apartment. "It has the space I'll need, a small kitchen, bedroom, bath, and it's a reasonable price. It's perfect."

He pulls me into the apartment and shuts the door behind us. Jaw muscle jumping, his green eyes drill into me. "This is an *apartment*, Cass."

"Yes, it is." I tuck my phone into my purse, then meet his steady gaze. "Why are you here? I told you I'd be fine. Did your conference call end early?"

"I'm here because I want to know what the hell is going on. Is there something you want to tell me?" He looks at the space around us, his tone hardening. "No *project* needs all this. Are we done? Is this why you didn't want me to come? Why you haven't set a date?"

"Calder—"

A quick knock on the door cuts me off and the door swings open. "Cass, there you are. Oh—hello, I'm Judith Anders, the agent for this apartment," she says to Calder.

"Calder Blake," he says, shaking her hand. "Cass's fiancé."

Judith's brows elevate under her slash of dark bangs, her brown eyes dancing in delight. "You didn't tell me you were marrying a *Blake*, Cass. Looks like we won't need to get in touch with your father as Guarantor after all."

I bristle at her presumption. "Calder's not involved with this, Judith."

"But he can be," he interjects, his tone tight.

Ugh, I'm really making a mess of this. I meet his angry gaze with a determined one of my own, then continue, "What I mean is...this is for my business. I'm doing this transaction. Why can't we just use my own financials? That's at least twelve months rent. My old landlord has written a letter. Shouldn't that all be enough?"

Judith tucks the folder against her chest, then tilts her head slightly. "Well, if yours is the only financials, we're going to have a problem. Your income this last year has been erratic and then with the recent credit report I pulled, you probably won't qualify."

My cheeks flame at that hard smack in the face. It's especially embarrassing that Calder got to hear it. I can't bear to look his way. "What? That can't be right. Yes, there were a couple of credit card issues several months ago, but those were stolen. It wasn't me. I reported it. That shouldn't show up on *my* credit."

"What does show up is that they were opened under your name and it was more than a couple, Cass. Unfortunately, the amount of credit cards being opened, and the length of time before the issue of fraud is reported, all that does effect your credit score."

"I only have one card. How many more? Ugh, looks like I'll be calling my credit card company again." *This is a nightmare.* "What about my Dad's financials from when I got my last apartment?"

"Your father's information will need to be updated. I tried to call and get his consent to use him as Guarantor once more, but the phone has been disconnected."

I frown. "Disconnected? He's out of the country, but his phone should still go through to voicemail."

Judith nods. "I tried to call his office number and got the same thing."

"That's not possible. There's been some kind of mistake." Suddenly concerned for my parents, I pull my phone from my purse and dial our home phone number.

When the distinct "disconnected number" tone rings in my ear, I look at Calder, then quickly dial my father's office phone.

As the same dead tone echoes across the line, Calder steps beside me and wraps his arm around my waist. "She's covered, Judith. But she won't be taking this apartment."

"What?" I hang up and frown at him as he gestures to the windows.

"It's a first floor apartment, Cass. I won't support you in a place that isn't secure."

"Support me?" I'm starting to get annoyed. "I didn't ask for your support."

When his mouth presses in a firm line, Judith clears

her throat. "Why don't you two talk and we can reschedule?"

I start to speak, but Calder answers, "Sounds good. We'll be in touch."

Judith smiles and turns to the door, pulling it open. "Just flip the lock before you walk out."

I wait until Judith leaves the building before I round on him. "You had no right to interfere. I told you that I had it handled."

His expression hardens. "So when you asked your agent to use your father as Guarantor, you knew that your parents' home and business numbers were disconnected? Or that yet more credit cards have been opened in your name?"

His blunt comments sting. My parents had been so busy preparing for their three month long safari trip, I hadn't gone to see them, but my father would've *told* me if there was an issue with his business. I know he would've. "I'm sure there's some logical explanation for my parents' phones. I remember Dad mentioning a service he planned to hire. Some wires probably got crossed somewhere, disconnecting his phones instead of forwarding. I'll deal with the credit card issue, but *this* is exactly why I didn't want you to come. You completely took over. I want to do this myself."

"By using your dad as Guarantor?"

"It's not like he's ever *needed* to cover me," I huff, frowning.

Calder's expression softens slightly. "I will always protect you, Cass. If you had asked for my help, the financing wouldn't have come into question. For that matter, you don't even need to work."

It's my career. I built it. I don't want to depend on anyone else to keep it. I need it to be strong. *It might be all I ever have.* Calder's completely missing the point. The last thing I want to do is fight about this. I need to clear my head, so I walk out of the apartment and open the building's main door. Intending to head toward the train, I mumble, "I'm taking the train. I'll see you in a bit."

"My car's right here." Clasping my wrist, Calder steps in front of me as he closes the building's door. "You didn't answer my question earlier. You've dragged your feet setting a wedding date, and now this?" His expression tightens. "Why did I bust my ass getting the house in good shape if we're done? Are you moving out? What the hell is going on?"

"No, Calder." I shake my head quickly, folding my hand around his. "Everything is fine. I just need my own space to meet with clients and work on special shoots, so I can rebuild my photography business that I've let go this last year. My books and the freelance jobs I've done for BLACK Security only bring in so much income. I have to figure out how to rekindle my career, while trying not to travel every week..." I sigh at his instant frown. Yep, he'd hate that. "To do that I'll need a place in the city with enough room to work. And before you say it...your place near Gil's gym doesn't have enough space or natural light." Rubbing my temple, I look away.

"You don't need a place with a bedroom." His tone is clipped as he pulls me close. Sliding his hand under my hair, he clasps my neck and thumbs my chin up so I have to meet his gaze. "There's only one bed you're sleeping in."

My heart thumps, sending my pulse racing. Why does his intense gaze and his masculine smell do this to me every time? The moment he dips his head to press his lips to mine, someone calls out, "Calder Blake!"

A tall, thick-boned man, and a shorter guy, hop out of a van parked on the street, cameras in hand. Another guy with thinning dark hair stops his car in the road and leans out his window, his camera already snapping. "I heard a rumor you're a guest speaker at Alana Shane's publisher's party celebrating her InkArt book hitting the USA Today," the burly guy from the van says. "Is it true? Will we see you at The Climb in SoHo tomorrow?"

"Alana says you two had a past relationship," Thin-haired car guy says. "Care to comment?"

Calder slits an annoyed gaze on the paparazzi. "Meet my fiancée, Cass Rockwell."

While the two men try to step in front of the guy in

the car to get a better shot with their cameras, they all fling questions my way.

"Where did you two meet?"

"Let's see that ring!"

"When's the wedding?"

"Are you pregnant?"

"That's enough," Calder barks. Wrapping his arm around my waist, he escorts me to his car parked directly in front of the building. I don't argue, because I want to get out of there as fast as possible. I remember seeing the paparazzi buzzing around Sebastian and Talia a few times, especially during her book signings. Once the whole Celeste ordeal settled, I'd been able to pretty much fly under the radar.

But now that these guys know I'm engaged to Calder, they'll be like a swarm of bees buzzing around us.

I block the camera's view with my hand so they can't capture how upset I am. I don't want them to see that I just learned about Calder's plans for tomorrow night with his ex-girlfriend splattered all over tomorrow's tabloid newsstands.

The fact Calder didn't immediately deny the rumor once we're alone in the car, tells me it's true. Since Calder doesn't say a word while he drives, I send off a quick text to my father asking about their phones, then call my credit card company and threaten to cancel my card with them if they can't guarantee to protect my account from getting hacked.

Once I hang up, I spend the rest of the ride home getting more annoyed at being blindsided by the media. Of *course* Alana turned her "tattoo portfolio" into a book. And of *course* it sold enough copies to hit the USA Today list. Fuck me. *Can I feel like even more of a failure right now?* Nope, not really.

As we pull up the drive, I can't hold it in any longer. "You have a lot of nerve getting upset with me about making a stupid appointment with an agent, while you're off making party plans with your ex."

Before he can reply, I get out and let myself in the house.

Stepping around drop cloths and paint cans in the kitchen, I punch the alarm code to stop it from beeping.

"She just called me today. I was going to tell you about the event tonight. I hoped you'd want to go with me." I tense at Calder's voice right behind me. He clasps my shoulder and turns me around, his gaze is hard and not at all regretful. "I'm doing a friend a favor for *one* evening. You intended to sign a contract that could keep you in town for who knows how many nights a week. That's usually something couples who're planning to marry discuss, but I wasn't even on your radar. Just like setting a fucking wedding date hasn't been."

"That's not true! I said we'd set it soon." *I think about*

you every minute...about how I don't want to fail you too. There's a lot I want to say, but until I hear back from the doctor, I don't want to unnecessarily add to Calder's frustration with his family history. Especially after learning he's having issues with Ben at work. I know where his anger is stemming from. Telling him he won't be able to start his own family line with me is the last thing he needs to hear right now. But none of that negates the fact that I'm still ticked about being caught off guard. I fold my arms, ready for battle. It's been a hell of a day for me too. "I'm not the one going around making dates with my exes."

"Stop calling it a date. It's an obligation." Grunting, he rakes a hand through his hair. "When she took the photos of my Steel tattoo for her temporary tattoo section, she mentioned that she might submit it for publication. I joked that if she did and it hit a list, I would help her promote it." He snorts as he tugs at his tie to pull the knot apart. "I never expected it to actually happen."

Now I'm even more irritated that she seemed to have lucked into hitting a list. The more I learn about this whole Alana situation, the crappier I feel. I refuse to have her success rubbed in my face for an entire evening. "Well, good for her. I won't be going to the event," I say, then start to walk around him to head upstairs.

"Saturday sounds good," he says in a firm tone.

I pause and look up at him, my heart starting to hammer. "What about Saturday?"

"For our wedding." He faces me, his gaze full of serious intent.

"No." I shake my head in a fast jerk. "There's not enough time—"

"For what? You to change your mind?" His face darkens and he steps into my personal space. "Damn straight, there's not."

"But my parents aren't here."

"Your parents adore me." He slides a hand intimately into my hair as if he didn't just plan a big life event for us to happen a few days from now. "They'll understand. And we can always have a celebration party later."

"You can't just set the date for this weekend, Calder. There's tons to do." I stutter as his gaze drops to my lips. "Pl—places to reserve."

His fingers tighten around my hair, keeping me from moving as his gaze snaps back to mine. "Do you get wet whenever I touch you?"

The intensity in his stormy green stare liquefies every muscle in my body. My fingers itch to run through his light-brown hair, then pull him close so I can feel his muscles press against me. Why does he have to be so freaking hot? I work hard to keep my voice even as his other hand moves under the edge of my dress, his fingertips grazing the front of my thigh. "Of course I do, but—"

"Does your body ache when I do this?" He grips my inner thigh, his thumb sliding so intimately close that I bite my lip to keep from moaning. When he presses down on the juncture of my leg, I hold my breath in anticipation. He has to feel the heat radiating off me.

Yes, damn it! "Does yours?" I grab hold of his belt. My fingers tease his goody trail, then dip past his underwear to barely brush the tip of his erection.

With a low growl, he fists my hair and tilts my head back. The moment our mouths align, he bites my bottom lip hard enough to make my legs shake. Releasing my lip, he slides his nose along my cheek. "Every time you so much as breathe in my direction, I'm instantly hard."

I let out an involuntary pant. I'm so revved and ready for his touch, my fingers instinctively tighten around his belt buckle. I want to yank the damn thing off, but I can't let him know how desperate I am. He'll use that knowledge to get me to agree to his crazy plan.

Warm breath bathes my jaw while his thumb slowly runs down the front of my damp underwear. Just one touch, but no more. *Ahhh, the torture.* I will not beg for it, no matter what he does. I will *not*. Yet I can't keep my hips from moving closer.

"Your sweet pussy is dripping for me, angel."

The man's completely unapologetic in his arrogance. "It's been a while," I counter, even as I fold my free hand around the back of his neck to pull him closer. I'm surprised he doesn't remind me that it's only been since last night, but then his voice drops to a carnal, knowing purr.

"How hard do I make you come, Cassandra Rockwell?"

So hard. So many times. Oh God, stop the torment. "Just touch me!"

He curls his fingers around the back of my head and yanks me fully against him, rasping in my ear with a rough, demanding grate. "Then you'd better fucking set a date, Raven-mine."

While part of me wants to rail at him, my fingers still dig into his hair, keeping him close. "We can decide next week. I promise."

Calder stiffens and pulls back to scowl at me. "I want an answer now."

"Next week will be perfect." Panic makes my stomach tumble. "You—you'll be happier once I can scout out a few places and know our plan."

"I'll be happier?" He jams his hands into his hair, eyes blazing with fury. "Why does everyone keep telling me what *I* want? I know my own mind, goddamnit!" Narrowing his gaze on me, he continues, "But apparently I'm the only one who does."

I've never seen him this angry. As hard as it is to stay silent, I realize I was right to keep quiet until I can confirm with the doctor. My hand shakes as I put it on his chest. "Calm down, Calder. You know I love you."

"Do you?" he says, stepping back so my hand falls. "Because you sure as hell have a funny way of showing it."

I know he's lashing out in frustration, but it's hard not to take it personally.

"You have no idea how much I'm trying not to scream at you right now," I say in an even tone.

"Then do it!" he snaps.

"The way you're acting...this anger...it isn't just about us, Calder. Something else is going on." When he doesn't speak, but just scowls at me, I try to draw it out of him. "What's with the blow up with Ben today?"

"He pushed too far," he says, folding his arms.

"This is beyond him just being an annoyance. What did he say that upset you so much?"

Calder shrugs. "Nothing that matters."

Yeah, right. His gaze has already shuttered. Whenever it comes to his half-brother, blinders go up. "I've seen Ben trying to joke with you, and you just won't have any of it. I wish you'd let down your guard a little and give him a chance. He's a good guy if you'd just—"

"Why?" he grates, his arms falling to his sides. "Why do you keep pushing him on me?"

"Because he's your brother. You have no idea what I would give if I could have Sophie back. The bond we had was immeasurable. I know the team at BLACK Security is awesome, but also surrounding yourself with those who'll have your back despite your differences is important. That's what family does, Calder. When it comes down to it, blood *is* thicker than water."

"Fuck Phillip for all of it! And fuck Ben too," he barks. "What I *need* is my own family, Cass. Not Sebastian, not my other cousins, or the team at BLACK Security. Call me old-fashioned, but I would like your last name to be Blake *before* junior comes along."

I blink back the cloud of mist in my eyes. He's had such a rough year after learning his mother committed suicide because of what Phillip did to her, then finding out that raging psychopath was also his biological father. I understand his struggle, but the past won't change, no matter how much we wish it could. It's how we move toward our future that dictates who we become. Calder couldn't be any clearer in his desire to start a family, and the last thing I want to do is disappoint him on that front too.

"You've got nothing to say?"

I nod and swallow the painful lump in my throat. Thinking quickly to buy myself some time, I gesture to the paint paraphernalia around us. "The house is nearly done and all this stuff will be cleared out this weekend, right? We'll start working on wedding plans next week once it's gone. Hopefully we'll be able to book a church on such short notice, and the florist and caterers. Then there's the reception location. If we can't book that, we might have to wait just a little bit..."

He stares at me, then says curtly, "I need some air," before he walks out of the house.

When his car engine roars to life, I grab the doorknob and open it, but he's already backed out and the garage door is going down.

Closing me off. Just like that.

My heart races as I panic and retrieve my phone from my purse. We've never fought. Not like this. Disagreed, yes. One would stalk away and the other would follow. We talked. We worked it out, but this...

I try to type in my password, but my hands are shaking so bad I can't get the passcode to work. When I finally get it typed in correctly, my phone screen display goes completely black as my phone dies.

"Why won't this phone keep its charge?" I growl at the stupid phone, then whisper, "He'll be back," to calm myself down. *But where is he going?* When my gaze lands on the duffle bag that he normally takes with him when he goes to the gym, my heart sinks. *Where else would he go? Would he go see Alana?*

The possibility makes me scan the island quickly, looking for my charger. *Where is it?* When I don't spot it underneath yesterday's mail, I run into the library that doubles as an office and pull open the main desk drawer to find one of Calder's. My gaze snags on a manila envelope and I stop searching to open it. Big tears cloud my vision as dozens of small baggies, full of cut up pictures, fall out onto the desk. Calder didn't get rid of all of his family photos like I thought he had. Even though they're in pieces, he'd kept some. Sniffling, I pick up a few of the baggies, feeling hopeful as an idea comes to me.

He'll calm down and come home, but a project will keep my mind occupied. I'll just need a few supplies.

As soon as I get in my car and see my charger on the passenger side floorboard, I roll my eyes and plug it into the car and my phone, then start the engine. My heart lifts when a text instantly buzzes through, but the excitement fades that it's not from Calder.

A blocked number.

Secret keepers have an obligation to keep their secrets safe. Are you going to make me come to you?

Well shit...there's no way *that* text was sent to the wrong person. This is Celeste's secret, not mine, so what does she mean by that? Is she in some kind of trouble? I quickly glance behind me at the open garage door, my heart racing. The last thing I want her to do is show up at Calder's house. If someone recognized her, we'd all be in hot water. Worse, Phillip's jail time could be reduced. I chew on my bottom lip and glance at my watch, trying to decide what to do.

Calder would insist that I stay the hell away, but all I can picture is the look of betrayal on Beth's face if she found out that her sister was not only alive but needed help and I ignored her. At least for now, the burden of checking on Celeste and her baby falls on me. I grimace at the text. *Keeping secrets sucks.*

Even though the text just came through...it says it was sent a couple hours before. Stupid phone. It's definitely time to get a new one. Instead of replying, I pull out of our driveway and turn in the direction of the library.

I cut the engine in the parking lot of our old high school and check the time. Almost five. The library will close in seven minutes.

Luckily, I don't have to waste time getting a visitor's badge because the main doors are thrown open. *Probably to air out the high school funk.* I smirk at the thought and head for the library.

Once there, I go straight to the section where *Colored By Design* is kept. Celeste used this book before when she left behind a message confessing that she was very much alive and how she'd framed Phillip for what he'd done to her. The real kicker was that she thanked me because she couldn't have pulled it off without my help. Thinking about how she'd used me, I mutter quietly, "I can't believe I'm being dragged in again."

When I reach the slot on the shelf where the book would normally be, I'm surprised it's missing. I look all around on the shelf above, then below, but I don't see the oversized book on colors and design.

The sound of a book hitting the floor with a soft thump a couple aisles over, draws my attention.

I glance back to see if the librarian noticed the noise before I step over the footstool. Just as I peer around the bookshelf, I catch a quick glimpse of the back of a guy with short dark hair, a dark colored shirt, and faded jeans before he disappears down that aisle.

I move quickly over to the section I'd seen him enter, but by the time I peek around the edge, no one's in that aisle.

Quickly walking over to the desk, I speak to the mid-twenties librarian in a black bob with teal streaks on either side of her face. "Excuse me. Did you see the guy who just left?"

She looks up from scanning the bar code in the back of a returned book and shakes her head. "I didn't, but even this late in the day students have been known to flit in and out of here without checking out a thing. Is there something I can help you with?"

Shaking off the feeling he's watching me, I nod. "Can you please let me know if you have *Colored By Design* in your return stack behind the desk?"

She looks at her stacks of returned books, then taps out the name of the book on her computer. "Ooh, that's an old one. I'm surprised they haven't retired it. Are you sure it's not on the shelf?"

"No, it's not there. I checked all around and didn't see it."

"Then I guess someone checked it out but it didn't get scanned. If you want, I can take your name and call you when it's returned?"

I shake my head. "That's okay. I'll just check back another time. Thanks for your help." *Why do I feel like I've just been played?* I can hear Calder now, grumbling in my ear, "See, I told you to stay out of it."

Whatever Celeste is cooking up, I want no part of it. Walking out of the library, I reply to Celeste's last text.

I kept your secret. That's where my obligation ends. Do not contact me again.

CHAPTER FIVE

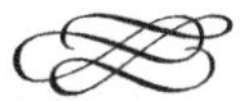

CALDER

I drove for a while trying to calm down, but I couldn't settle, so I found myself heading for Gil's gym. Even though Gil lives upstairs, since the lights are on down in the gym, I stop in. It's quiet when I open the main door, but that doesn't surprise me considering the late hour.

Gil's been a gruff mentor and pretty much a second dad to me since my father passed away. Volunteering at his gym and teaching MMA techniques mixed with my own SEAL skills is the least I can do to repay him for helping me get past my father's death. Not to mention, it's rewarding work to see these guys channel their personal demons into something positive.

Normally I'd work out my frustrations on the mat, but I left my gear at home, so when I don't see Gil in his office,

I head for the gym. It's storming out and the scent in the room is a mixture of rain, sweat, and pine disinfectant. No one's around, except a thin kid who looks to be about fourteen or so. He's standing with his back to the door and shadow boxing his reflection in the window, arms flying like a hummingbird.

It's hard not to chuckle at all the energy he's exerting. But when he turns slightly and the look on his face registers, my amusement quickly dies. Sweat shines against his dark temples, eyes full of intense fire, mouth pressed in a thin line, and forehead pinched in focused concentration; this kid's fighting for his life.

"Is Gil here?"

He whips around, his brown gaze slitting in suspicion. "Who's asking?

"I'm Calder." I unbutton my jacket to look more relaxed so he doesn't feel threatened and lift my chin toward his gloved hands raised in front of his face. "I saw a lot of hooks, crosses and uppercuts. Work more on your jabs."

"Jabs are for weaklings." He snorts as he looks my custom suit up and down. "Why should I listen to you?"

He's got a lot of attitude, his gaze instantly distrusting. Probably why he's here. It boils my blood to see someone so young feel that threatened. He's the youngest person I've seen at Gil's gym by far. I step into the room, but stop when he takes a step back. "Jabs exert the least amount of energy since the fist you're using is the closest to your opponent. They also help you gauge his skills while setting you up for the big punches."

He tilts his head, doubt in his eyes. "*You* do MMA?"

"I dabble." Sliding my hands into my pockets, I nod toward his feet. "Keep your lead foot and toes facing the same direction as your chest and hips. Unless you're blocking knees, then turn your foot forward so you can check."

The boy sets up like I suggested, then does a couple of punches and a knee check move. "Like this?"

I nod. "Be sure to switch up your angles. Don't always come in from the same direction." He complies and I smile. "Yeah, pivot like that, but try not to slide your feet when you move around. Stay on your toes. You'll move much faster that way."

"He's got some good pointers, David." Gil's gruff voice rumbles, his cane thumping the mat's edge as he moves into place beside me.

"I guess." David shrugs off his interest and removes his gloves. "He's no Steel. That guy's legendary." Hope fills his gaze as he looks at Gil. "Do you think I'll ever get to meet him?"

"Maybe he'll come by one day." Gil's gaze cuts to me for a second before he looks at the kid once more. "Don't you have an exam tomorrow? I've got some paperwork to take care of, then I'll be up."

David looks at me and smiles slightly. "Um, thanks for the tips. Maybe I'll see you around?"

I nod. "Nice to meet you, David. Next time I'll bring my gloves."

His eyes light up and his smile widens. "To spar?" When Gil clears his throat, David looks sheepish. "Okay, okay...I'm going."

"It appears things have changed a lot around here while I've been buried in house repairs," I say as I follow Gil to his office.

"You could say that, *Steel*."

When I smirk at him, he grunts and closes his office door, then moves behind his desk.

While I take the seat in front of his desk, he says, "He kept coming by the gym. Hanging around at all hours. When I figured out he was homeless, I offered him a place to stay, but only if he worked for me and spent some of his pay enrolling in community college."

I blink. "He can't be more than fifteen."

Gil shakes his head. "He's actually eighteen. Just severely malnourished with a horrible background to go with it. The kid is crazy smart but hasn't realized that yet about himself."

I set my jaw. "Then I'm glad he found you. No one will whip him into shape faster."

Gil grunts his agreement, then quickly swipes his cane across the desk and points it directly at me. "What's going on? I didn't expect to see you back here for at least another week. Did they finish your renovations early?"

"Believe it or not, that's finally almost done." The last thing I want to do is talk about how much Ben pisses me off. And I sure as hell don't want to discuss Phillip at all. Rubbing the back of my neck, I grumble. "I've just got other frustrations going on."

Gil's weathered face wrinkles with a doubtful squint as he lowers his cane to the desk. "Remodeling can be a pain in the ass for sure, but I've never known you to get bent out of shape over stuff like that. And I know this can't have anything to do with that angel you're marrying. So what's bugging you?"

My mouth tightens. "Guess I've got an angel problem then."

"More likely it's all in your head," Gil says, snorting.

I let my frustration over the apartment and Cass not setting a date pour out, but the last thing I expected is to watch Gil's face shift from a frown to a scowl as I talk.

"Why did you tell her that she doesn't need to work?"

Why is he asking me that while I'm trying to figure out how to get her to set a fucking date? "Because it's the truth. This is about Cass not committing, Gil. It's about me working my ass off to get our house ready in record time for *us* and not only is she off looking at another property, but she seems no closer to setting a date than the day I put a ring on her finger."

Gil clears his throat and lifts his hat from his desk, slipping it on his salt and pepper curly hair. "By commenting about her not having to work, you pretty much dismissed her entire career and the effort she's been going through to salvage it."

"What?" I sit up straight in the chair. "That's not what I said."

"I guarantee that's how it came across...intentional or not. Working *is* her choice, and you should not only support her decision, but encourage it." Leaning back in his chair, Gil crosses his arms. "And then you went for a walk because she wouldn't commit to a date at your insistence?"

It sounds kind of bad when he says it like that. "I'm just frustrated, Gil. She's stalling. I have no idea why, but she is. I don't know how to convince her to just set a date. It shouldn't be this hard." Raking my hand through my hair, I shake my head.

"So what if she is stalling? What exactly are you afraid of?"

That my asshole half-brother might be right and she's having second thoughts. I raise my eyebrow. "Why do you ask that?"

"Even good marriages have their ups and downs," Gil says, rubbing the silver scruff on his jaw. "But if you really love this woman, then give her the space she needs.

There's a reason she hasn't set a date. When she's ready, she'll tell you why."

"I'm not good at waiting." I shake my head, frowning. "As far as I'm concerned, I've been a fucking saint up until now."

"Well, tough nuts." He holds his hand up when I start to argue. "I might not have been married myself, but my parents had the best marriage until the day they died. Want to know what their secret was?" He waits until I raise my eyebrows. "They never, ever went to bed mad. They'd stay up until the wee hours and hash it out if they needed to." Pointing at me, he grunts. "*That* is how you keep your relationship going. You work on it. Every. Single. Day. As for the house stuff, it doesn't matter whether it's a tiny city apartment or a ten-thousand square foot estate, both are just walls and a roof over your head. A *home* is where the person who makes you happy resides. That's what you protect at all costs."

As annoyed as I am that he thinks I'm completely wrong, I can't help but smirk at the irony. "I can't believe a confirmed bachelor just gave me marriage advice."

He picks up his cane and stands. "Just doing my job of saving you from yourself. My knowledge comes from my own family dynamic and a few decades of watching friends go through divorces. Now get your ass out of here and go apologize to your fiancée."

CHAPTER SIX

CASS

My eyes fly open as a loud boom of thunder shakes the house. Harsh wind howls, lashing rain against the windows and hammering in heavy sheets down on the rooftop.

Sitting up on the couch, I blink in the pitch dark to clear my sleep-grogged head. *What time is it?* I grope blindly for my phone on the coffee table, but when I don't find it, I glance in the kitchen at the oven clock. Completely black.

Great, the storm must've knocked the power out. It could be seven or eleven. I stand and turn, trying to figure out why something feels off. As the rain and thunder continue their loud din, it hits me what's bothering me. There's no lightning. Not a single flash has happened since I woke up. Which right now would help me see more than a foot in front of me.

I hold my hands out and blindly follow the loud rain sounds. As soon as I turn the corner, I see the issue and rush forward. Rain is pouring into our open sliding glass patio door, drenching the carpet. The deluge soaks my clothes as I tug on the heavy door to close it. The moment it's fully shut, lightning briefly flashes and I jump at my own reflection in the glass.

Heart racing, I chuckle that I'd just scared the crap out of myself.

But the instant it hits me that my hair looks far wetter than it feels, the door starts to tug against my hold. I squeeze the handle as Celeste calls through the glass, "Open the door, Cass."

I don't know why, but I panic and quickly latch the door.

"I won't let you ignore me," she says, scowling.

Why is she here? I take a step back and call for Calder. *Where is he?*

Celeste raises her arm, her face livid. "Let me in!"

When I shake my head, she brings the backside of her fist down on the glass with shocking power. I scream for Calder as the booming hit cracks the glass. She growls her anger and hits it again, the force reverberating through me in deafening concussive waves that make me so dizzy, I'm unsteady on my feet. As my vision fades, I feel myself falling.

I BOLT upright on the couch, Calder's name still on my lips. Thunder booms and lightning flashes, briefly illuminating the dark room just as Calder rounds the coffee table. Crouching next to me, he brushes my hair away from my face, his hand warm against my clammy skin. "Are you okay? I just walked in and freaked when you called out my name. You sounded terrified."

"I must've fallen asleep." I lean into his comforting touch as I pick up my phone from the coffee table. "What time is it?" I mumble so he thinks that's why I'm checking the screen. *It was a dream.* Celeste didn't send any more texts. I exhale in relief.

Thunder vibrates the windows and Calder shakes his head as he slides his hand into my hair. "I can't believe you slept through all this racket." Pulling me forward, he kisses my forehead, then quickly looks at me with a worried gaze. "You're trembling."

"It was just a nightmare." Taking a steadying breath, I offer a wry smile. "I was dreaming about Celeste."

He instantly scowls. "Now I see why you called it a nightmare. Wonder why she's starring in your dreams after all this time?"

I sigh. Now that I've cut off all communication, I

might as well tell him about her text. "She tried to contact me today."

His expression hardens and his whole body tenses. "You didn't respond, did you?"

"Only to tell her not to contact me anymore." I don't need a lecture. It's over and done.

"Good," he says, visibly relaxing. "The last thing we need is Celeste returning from the dead. All hell would break loose."

"I completely agree." Wrapping my hand around his wrist, I adopt a calm expression and search his gaze in the darkness. "Are *you* okay?"

"I've just been spending too much time in my own head." He quickly scoops me up in his arms, his hold on me especially tight.

"What are you doing?" My heart races as I grip his broad shoulders. *Keep holding me tight, Calder. Promise to never let me go, no matter what.*

"Apologizing," Calder murmurs as he nuzzles my neck while carrying me upstairs. The thunder rumbles in a low bass and the rain rushes against the windows as we enter our darkened room.

I'm surprised that he doesn't lower me to my feet but instead sets me on the edge of our chaise lounge near the window. Lightning flashes as he towers over me and tilts my chin up. The churning of the storm just outside the window amplifies his heated gaze, spiking my adrenaline. As he begins to tug off his tie, I keep my gaze locked with his and wait for him to speak, but he doesn't say a word. He loops his tie around the scroll-work at the top of the lounge's back, then shrugs out of his jacket.

I'm so mesmerized as he unbuttons his dress shirt, that my gaze devours every inch of his gorgeous body as he peels the shirt away. From his six-pack abs to his broad chest, I'll never get tired of burying my face against his warm, muscular frame. For now I don't mind the silence between us. He's here. That's all that matters. We'll work through this.

When he lowers himself to his knees in front of me, my hand instantly traces the inked raven feathers curved around his left shoulder and down his bicep. "I love this raven wing so much," I say in a quiet voice. "I think it's wonderful that others will be able to appreciate this masterpiece in Alana's book, and that you're a man of your word."

Capturing my hand, he presses his lips to my palm in a slow tantalizing kiss. I take a shaky breath, trying not to get too emotional at how much he makes me feel with just a simple press of his lips to my skin. But he does. Every time, he melts me.

He bites down on the fleshy part of my palm, then flicks an intense gaze my way. "I will never apologize for wanting to make you mine."

My chest constricts. I love him so much. "You don't have to. I'm already yours."

"Not the same thing, angel." He bites me again, then rakes his teeth across the tender part of my wrist, before softly kissing my scars hidden underneath the ink. "I want every man to know you're taken, completely and permanently. The sooner the fucking better."

"I am fully and completely taken." I cup his jaw and make him look at me. "Next week, okay?"

I hold my breath as his gaze searches mine. I can tell he wants to question me more, but instead he nods and slides his hands up my thighs, pushing my dress out of the way. "You might want to hold on for this."

Before I can say a word, he grips my hips and turns me so fast, I fall against the back of the chaise.

My breath escapes in a gasp when he pushes my legs to the floor on either side of the chair, his voice gruff with want. "Keep them here for now."

Lightning flashes and thunder shakes the house as the summer storm announces its fury. It might be raging outside, but nothing compares to the tempest building in my body as Calder slides his thumbs under the thin straps at my hips, then rips my flimsy underwear completely off me.

When he yanks me forward, I yelp in surprise at his intensity and grope for something to hold on to as he looks at me like a starving man before he lowers his head to my sex. My hands connect with the silk tie he'd hooked to the back of the chaise and I grab onto it. Sliding my hand through the loop, I wrap the soft material around my wrist just as his mouth fully connects with my sensitive skin. The second his lips find my clit, I arch into his hot mouth and moan my pleasure, ready to give him every part of me.

I pant and grind against him, enjoying the sheer bliss he knows exactly how to provoke. If he insisted on setting a date while he was doing this, I would never be able to stand my ground.

Calder's grip tightens on my thigh and his fingers slide deep inside me as his mouth moves over me, encouraging my rapt participation. My heart races and twists with all the emotions rolling through me. This man is my tether. He makes me feel whole, even when I know I'm not.

Worry about my fertility jacks my emotional response and I hook my legs around his shoulders, desperately pulling him as close as he can get. *I love him so much. How fair would it be for me to bind him to me when he might not be able to have the family he needs to help him forget about the past?* The question echoes in my head over and over as my body spirals into a heart-shattering climax.

Once I scream through my orgasm, Calder doesn't stop. He keeps going until I've climaxed again. This time even harder. My legs are jelly and my heart is racing to keep up with the shudders of pleasure shooting through me.

"Enough, Calder," I finally beg him, truly afraid my body won't be able to handle another orgasm.

With a grunt of masculine pride, he moves up my body and lays his full weight on me. His erection pressing against me through his clothes, he clasps my face and rumbles against my mouth, "Damn, you fucking rule my world, angel."

"Not yet," I say with a breathless laugh, my heart still racing as I release the tie to wrap my arms around his thick shoulders. When his lips press hard against mine, I relish in the rough thrust of his tongue. Swirling mine around his, I roll my hips and make as much contact with his erection as possible. "But I promise it'll be memorable once you remove the rest of your clothes."

"Right now..." He pulls back, then stands and scoops me into his arms. Pressing his lips to my neck, he rumbles in a restrained tone, "We're going to talk."

I gulp my worry as he sets me on the bed and pulls on the string to unravel the bow at my shoulder. As the material falls and the upper part of my breast is revealed, I say, "Talking goes both ways."

Calder tugs on the other bow until the top half of my dress completely falls away. I hold my breath as he traces his fingers along the tip of my breast. "I said we're talking, so yes, that includes two people."

"But don't you want to...?" I'm not ready to stop. I want to feel him inside me. I need to feel that connection. I pull at his belt buckle and tug his belt off. When I reach for his zipper, Calder clasps my hand, his brow furrowed. "We're talking."

I'm not ready to talk and he's entirely too persuasive when we're in bed together. "Are you hungry? We can make a quick dinner."

"Just ate. Best damn meal every single time."

My face flames as he steps back from my hold and unzips his pants, his expression suddenly serious. "Take everything off and get in bed."

Tense with desire and anxious anticipation, I ignore the fluttering in my stomach and strip, then slide under the covers. Calder joins me, but when I try to wrap my arms around him, he quickly turns me around and tucks my body back against his hard chest. "Talking," he says sternly.

Lacing his fingers with mine, he folds our hands between my breasts, then presses his lips to the spot behind my ear. "I'm sorry I left. It was hard enough having my entire family ripped away from me, and I refuse to have another one shoved onto me in its place just because we share the same blood. You ground me, Cass. Without you, I'd have lost my shit when I learned about Phillip. Instead, I got to focus on us. On loving you and the future we'll build together with little Blakes running around driving us crazy like I did my parents." He chuckles and nuzzles my neck.

Oh, Calder... I blink the worried tears away and keep my tone light. "Can you imagine the kind of trouble our kids will get into with Sebastian and Talia's? It's a good thing Blakes are thick as thieves. I have a feeling they'll need to back each other up." *God, I want this tight knit family surrounding mine with love and protection, but there's no way I'm bringing up my fertility stuff right now.* That can wait until next week, so I kiss his knuckles and share the other issue bothering me.

"Everyone is in a good place with their careers. You and Sebastian have BLACK Security, you've got your volunteer time with Gil and the MMA group. Talia's now working with you, while continuing to write books, and I heard her on the phone the other day consulting with her old boss on a case he's investigating."

"She's such an overachiever."

I snort at his comment and sigh. "I'm serious. I just need to figure this out. Writing books about the city and the jobs Talia gives me will be side projects, but I want to take fashion photos again. Photography is my passion. It's in my blood. I just need to figure out how to do that and not travel twenty-four/seven. I love New York. I don't want to constantly be leaving it or you for work."

"I'm glad I'm second on that list."

I look at him over my shoulder. "You know what I mean."

"I know that I should always be *first* on your list," he says with a scowl. "And I also know that it's going to work out."

"How do you know that?" I wish I had his confidence. Mine's been rattled more than a few times lately.

Calder meets my gaze. "You were going to rent a place for a year without knowing exactly how it would work. If that's not ballsy, I don't know what is."

Even though I had just enough money in the bank to give myself twelve months to make it work, it was pretty freaking ballsy. "When you put it that way, I sound all kinds of crazy. Though I did just recently add this new app to my phone that will alert me about any social media posts on all my past clients as well as some big time bloggers in the industry. Between those two groups, hopefully I'll be able to start building leads for my business."

"Which will be?"

I finally voice a concept that has only existed in my head. "I built my business one client at a time to become a top fashion photographer, but I remember those early days starting off with just my one camera and gut instincts. So I want to do something that takes me back to my roots...or some variation of that." Scrunching my nose, I continue, "It doesn't sound like a lot, but hopefully I can turn my very loose concept into a feasible business plan."

"Other than traveling less, is there anything you did before that you would do differently now with this new business you want to start?"

I smile that he seems genuinely interested and feel less worried sharing a bit of my fears. "Well, one thing I realized is that I shouldn't have kept Raven anonymous. I should have released my New York City book under the Raven name with my picture in the bio and banked on her popularity to help boost sales. Instead, I released under my real name with no connection to Raven, and that made it harder for my book to be noticed. Lesson learned. Now that it's been a while since Raven has worked, I know it'll be a bit tougher climb back to the top when it comes to restarting my business, but I'm determined."

He taps my nose, then slides his fingers under my chin as he steals a kiss. "My fiancée is a smart, sexy, resourceful woman. I have no doubt she will make it work. All of it."

When I try to face him, Calder throws his leg over mine and tightens his arms around me. "Nuh..uh. Not so fast. To be continued next week."

I can clearly feel his erection nudging my butt cheek, but he's not releasing me, so I frown. "Enough joking."

"I'm not," he says, his expression resolute. "I'm waiting for the wedding date announcement."

When I start to giggle, then cackle uncontrollably, Calder frowns. "You don't think I can do it?"

I inch back against his hard cock and snicker when he

lets out an involuntary groan. "Nope. I really don't think you can, Mr. Sexy-Stick."

"My resolve is rock solid." He releases my hand and runs his fingertips lightly along the edge of my breast then down toward my nipple, his movements slow and sensual. "And I can't wait to unlock *all* your secrets."

I tense at his casual comment, then realize he's referring to our sex life, but I hold onto that tension to keep from reacting to his touch. The closer his fingers get to my nipple, the harder it gets not to respond. Just before he connects and sends my heart racing all over again, I grasp his hand. "I'm certainly not giving you the key, Master Puzzler. No sex, no touching."

"I never said anything about no touching. Your skin is so soft. You know I like to fall asleep holding you."

I hide a secret smile. I can count on one hand the number of times he hasn't fallen asleep cupping my breast. Rolling out of his hold and onto my side to face him, I toss my long hair over my shoulder and rest my head on my pillow as I meet his frustrated gaze in the darkness. "If you're going to insist on this ridiculous celibacy, then you'll have to go cold turkey. Those are my terms."

"But—"

"Nuh...uh. Next week, handsome."

He frowns, then his expression settles. "How about a concession for tonight considering I rocked your world?"

I bite my lip, feeling a tad guilty, but then again, it's not my fault he decided on waiting until next week.

"Fine," I say and lift his hand.

Calder flashes a grin briefly until I set his palm on the curve of my hip. "There," I say, patting the back of his hand. "You're holding onto me. Night, night, Navy."

While his eyes glitter with retribution in the darkness, I just go about my business fluffing my pillow. Exhaling, I close my eyes, then yelp when I'm jerked forward until my head lands on his pillow, my breasts are smashed against his hard chest, and my fiancé's hand is firmly clamped on my bare ass.

"That's much better," he says in a lion's purr of satisfaction.

Two can play at this game. I slide my leg between his and pull myself fully against his erection. It's sweet torture to feel his heat and hard body so close, but I squirm against him and act like I'm just getting comfortable. I gasp when Calder clamps his teeth on that sweet spot between my neck and shoulder, then inwardly shudder with want as he rumbles his dominance in my ear, "Enough, Cassandra!" Kissing my forehead, he grabs my ass once more in an even more possessive hold, his tone rough and husky. "Night, angel."

"Night," I grudgingly mumble.

Unlike Calder, I can't fall asleep right away. I lay there pressed against his warmth, feeling safe, protected, and very much wanted. Despite his declaration of abstinence, my heart aches with so much love for this man—maybe even a little more because of it. Not that I would ever tell him that. I inhale his masculine scent and press a kiss to his jaw, then snuggle even closer and whisper over and over in my head, "It'll all be okay," until Calder's rhythmic breathing lulls me to sleep.

CHAPTER SEVEN

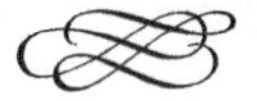

CASS

"Morning, sleepy head." Calder leans over and kisses me awake.

"Not yet," I mumble sleepily and start to *shoo* him away, then come fully awake when his cologne wafts over me and I remember what I missed out on last night. Just as I try to wrap my arms around his neck and convince him what a bad idea his abstinence is, he straightens and sets my phone on the nightstand.

"I just wanted to say goodbye and leave you your phone."

I'm sad that he's already showered and dressed, so I watch him button his black suit jacket with a mixture of admiration and regret. "You look especially handsome this morning."

"Apparently abstinence really *does* make the heart grow fonder," he says with a smug smile as he straightens his black tie.

And far too chipper for someone who went to bed without last night. "That's *absence* by the way." Leaning on my elbow, I brush my bedhead hair back. "Why such a formal suit today? Are you meeting with a special client?"

"I have a full day ahead. Lots of meetings, so I'll be heading to Alana's event straight from work."

He's dressing up for it? *Grrrrr.* As annoyed as I am, I keep my expression carefully composed and shrug. "Oh, okay. See you tonight then."

"Yep, the event starts at seven." He turns and heads for the doorway. "I'll send you all the details."

"Wait!" I quickly sit up and walk forward on my knees. "I'm not goin—" Something sharp jabs into my knee. Wincing, I glance down to a familiar oversized book digging into my skin. *Colored by Design.* My gaze jerks to the doorway. "Where did this come from?"

Calder turns in the doorway. "The package was sitting on the front porch when I went out to check the mail we missed getting last night." He grins and glances down at the book. "Going old school with your photography ideas, huh? Retro is always hot. Got to go. See you at the club, angel. Just give them your name at the door."

I'm too shocked by the book stabbing into my knee to remind him that I'm not going.

Tucking my legs underneath me, I stare at the book and bite my lip. If only I had known that leaving me her confession letter was Celeste's way of staying tied to her old life, I never would have gone to that library. *Now what do I do with this Pandora's box?*

Why is she insisting on this mode of communication? It made sense when I was in her house and the phone she gave me could have been bugged by Phillip. "I'm not opening it, Celeste," I mutter. "I am *not* playing into your games."

As if in response to my adamant statement, a text comes through on my phone. I'm almost afraid to look, but at least then I can tell Celeste that sending me the book won't change a thing. I grab my phone to text her just that, but the message is from Beth.

I'm here at the estate doing some stuff for my father. The house feels so empty. Why is this massive sense of loss hitting me now instead of when I attended my mom's funeral? Or Celeste's? I miss my sister and mom. It's like a hole is growing in my chest and I don't know how to make it stop. Thanks for offering to listen. I appreciate your friendship so much.

Poor Beth. I close my eyes and tap my phone against my forehead several times. I'm only smarter in hindsight if other people would stop depending on me. Ugh, I have to know what Celeste needs.

With my sense of honor and responsibility kicking me

in the gut, I set my phone down and pull the book close, then open it to the same place Celeste had left me her confession letter last year. This time, a key joins the memory stick that slides out from the return card pouch in the back of the book. I quickly retrieve my laptop, slip the encrypted memory stick in the USB slot, then type my name as the password.

Dear Cass,

I need your help to keep a roof over my head. I planned carefully for my escape from my life, but I didn't plan on having health problems, which have left me with insane bills, some of which are already past due. I stockpiled an emergency fund in the wine cellar at the Carver Estate. The wine rack closest to the door has a raised bottom in the last drawer. The money is hidden underneath it. For obvious reasons, I can't get to the cash myself. I need you to get it and bring it to the address I've listed at the bottom of this letter. If I don't pay my rent by noon tomorrow, I'll be evicted. I'm pretty sure you don't want me to show up at your door.

No shit! I shudder as the memory of my nightmare flits through my mind. Shrugging it off, I continue reading.

These instructions must be followed exactly. When you come tomorrow, if I'm not there, you can just let yourself in the house, put the money and key in the lockbox on the table, then turn the bottom lock on the doorknob on your way out. You've kept my secret, so I trust you'll continue to do so, but the only way I can guarantee that no one will ever learn where I live is if you come alone. If you do this for me, I should be okay, and I promise to never contact you again. Destroy this letter once you've memorized the address and keep the book since you were so attached to it in high school. Honestly, it's not like anyone's going to miss that old relic.

Celeste

Giving up the book means she knows she won't have an untraceable way to communicate with me after this. Which means she plans to keep her word. I glance at the address, then look up the city name, Beacon. It's some small town outside of New York. I can't believe she's been less than two hours away this whole time. But why didn't Celeste mention her baby? Is her child all right? Oh God, did something go wrong and she lost the baby because she was so sick? I feel horrible that I was just going to blow her off. Still, the part of me that has been burned by Celeste in the past pushes me to read over her letter again with a skeptical eye.

After I scan the letter once more, I take a deep breath and wonder what to do. Not once did Celeste plead for my help. She told me what she needed and expected it to be done. She didn't even thank me at the end. She made sure to play on my emotions about her health and dire financial straits, but what if she's not really sick?

What if she's just been living the high life, blowing through all her money, and now she's using me to get more from her family? But if she's telling the truth...how in the hell am I supposed to just waltz into the Carver's house and retrieve that money?

While my conscience wars with my own sense of self-preservation, it occurs to me that there might be a way to confirm Celeste's poor health. Well, the state of her health last year before she disappeared. Once I know if that part of her story is true, then I'll decide what to do next.

Grabbing my phone, I text Beth.

I'm so sorry, Beth. I'm sure it's hard being there alone. How about we eat lunch together again? I can bring whatever you'd like. It'll be nice to visit the estate as ME for once.

Awww, you're the best Cass! Father's out of town on business, so we'll have the place to ourselves. Well...and the staff. I've tried to convince him to sell it and move into the city, but he prefers things the way they are. Does noon work for you? Don't worry about bringing food, I'll order Vicci's in. I know it's your favorite.

Thanks. I'll see you then.

Thank you for being such an awesome friend. Truly.

Hopping out of bed, I head for the shower. Before I go see Beth, I really need answers about her sister.

CHAPTER EIGHT

CALDER

I really dislike back-to-back meetings. I'd rather be out in the field right now. So I find myself wandering into Bash's office while I wait for the next meeting to start, because sometimes a little levity makes the whole day better.

"What are you doing?" Bash drills me after he hangs up from his call.

Sliding my hands from my pants' pockets, I pull my attention from the long wall in his office and meet his blue gaze. "I had a few minutes before my next meeting, so I'm taking mental measurements. For when I win the bet."

He doesn't miss a beat as he picks up a stack of papers. "You haven't even set a date yet."

"We're going to next week. Then this space..." I spread my arms. "It'll be all mine."

"If you think for one minute that she'll make it through the actual wedding without saying the word traditional..." He snorts his confidence. "You really are deluded, Cald."

"I can pretty much guarantee it." I nod even as my balls still ache from last night's sexual sabbatical, but I'm damned determined to keep up my end of this abstinence deal. "So far nothing she's done comes even close to traditional. Hell, you wouldn't believe what it took to get her to commit to setting a date next week."

"I'll pass on the details," he mutters in a droll tone, then nods toward the door that connects his office to Talia's. "You planning on becoming Talia's officemate too?"

"Sure, why not?" I shrug, enjoying the look of annoyance spreading across his face. Just a bit of payback for yesterday. "Talia and I haven't worked together on a case. It might be fun to mix things up a bit."

Giving me a death glare, he snaps open the folder he'd picked up and pulls a paper out. "Speaking of schedules, here's yours for next week."

When I look down at the cases, I scowl. "What fresh hell is this? I'm with Hemming all fucking week. Yesterday's medical shit and now this? What happened to *equal* partners?"

"We rotate making the schedule," he says, closing the folder. "You did this week's. Next week is mine."

It takes everything inside me not to openly snarl at him, but I manage, barely. "You can't make me like him."

"You don't even know him. Get to."

"Or what?"

"I'll handcuff the two of you together and you can beat the ever-living shit out of each other," he snaps.

I flash a cold smile. "Fine by me."

Bash's gaze sharpens. "Then it's a good thing I make the schedule *half* the year."

"Goddamnit!" Crushing the paper, I pivot and walk out.

CHAPTER NINE

CASS

I'm thankful Calder doesn't look my way as he walks out of Sebastian's office. By the annoyed expression on his face, now wouldn't be a good time for him to learn the book left outside our house was from Celeste. But just like Talia always says, "A good investigator never jumps to conclusions. Check all the facts, then let your gut kick in for the rest." So, fact checking first.

Once I learn as much as I can about Celeste's health status, then I can decide what to do next. The hard part will be asking Talia for the information without revealing too much. Calder and I are the only ones who know that Celeste is still very much alive, and so long as Talia never learns the truth, she won't have to lie about it if asked under oath. I hate keeping this secret, but I must in order to protect everyone else from the backlash if the truth ever came out.

My heart jerks when Calder unexpectedly turns around, so I quickly step into Talia's office and pull the door nearly closed as he heads for Elijah's cubicle.

"Um, heya, Cass. Why are you sneaking around?" Talia calls from her desk.

Shutting the door, I give an apologetic half-smile. "Sorry, I was practicing getting out of the line of sight quickly."

Talia stands and re-tucks her silk blouse into her dove gray linen skirt, then comes around her desk. "So why are you still whispering?" she asks in a low voice.

"Oh, uh..." I exhale a nervous laugh and speak in a normal tone. "Still in stealth mode?" I say, irritated that my voice hitches.

"Okay, girlie." Talia snorts. "Spill it. Who are you trying to avoid?"

"I'm not trying to avoid Calder," I say quickly.

Her eyebrow arches. "I asked *who* you were trying to avoid. I never said Calder."

When I frown at her, she folds her arms. "Okay, fine," I say on a sigh. "I just want to get some information first before I share it with him."

"Does this have anything to do with yesterday's appointment that you didn't want Calder to attend?" As I gape, her green gaze turns serious. "Yeah, I noticed."

Talia doesn't miss a thing. "Actually, Calder showed up later, but the space didn't work out anyway." I grimace, accepting her softly spoken "oh no" with a nod. The last thing I want to do is blatantly lie to my best friend, so I skirt the truth about dodging Calder with a valid question.

"For a week or so now I've wondered if someone might be following me, or if it was just my imagination. I'm used to doing surveillance on specific locations or people in set places, so I have no point of reference when it comes to keeping up with a person. Before I mention this to Calder, I thought you could give me some pointers on how to spot a person who might be tailing me."

Talia picks up a print out and hands it to me. "I take it you haven't seen this." When my gaze drops to an article and picture from our local paper, she says, "Welcome to the family, Cass. Consider yourself lucky that you went this long before the media hounds plastered your picture all over town. They've probably been on you for a while just to get that shot."

"But they just discovered we were engaged yesterday..." I trail off and stare at the unhappy look on my face reflected between my open fingers, but it's the headline above the photo of Calder and me in the car that makes me grit my teeth. "Trouble in Paradise for Calder Blake and His Fiancée?" I toss the piece of paper onto her desk. "Ugh, really? Anything to sell a story, huh?"

She gives a sympathetic look. "I totally get it, so let's

go over a few pointers to make you feel comfortable. It's important that you know them for safety reasons anyway. Have a seat."

I sit in a chair at the small round table in the corner of her office.

"When it comes to the paparazzi, sunglasses are your friend, so are hats, hoodies, or anything that camouflages your normal look," she begins as she sits down across from me. "You've seen what I do to avoid them, so you're going to have to start using those methods. As for knowing if you're being followed, first off, you've always got your camera on you, so use it. Pretend to be snapping photos, but put your camera on burst mode and scattershot the whole area around you."

I nod. "Ah, that's a good idea."

She taps my phone that I'd set on the table. "Use this the same way. Flip it to your rear-facing camera and turn on record video, then hold your phone up to your ear and pretend to talk. As you walk around, turn like any normal person would while talking, except you'll be capturing the whole area around you."

I can't believe I didn't think to do that. I sit forward, completely rapt. "Ha, that's great. Using those techniques, I can prove I was being followed after the fact by reviewing images, but how can I confirm I'm being followed while it's happening?"

"Ah, okay...so in-the-moment stuff." Talia lifts her

hand and starts ticking off more pointers. "If you've seen the same person more than once in completely different areas, be on alert and in contact with us. Then start paying attention to things like: If the same person leaves the restaurant at the same time you do, or you see them flipping the pages of a book or magazine faster or slower than a normal person should, or they're stretching too long while out running. If anything sets off warning bells, move into a crowded area. Whether you're in a car or walking, stay where there are people. One way to confirm your suspicions is to take four different turns. If the person takes the same turns, they are more than likely following you. In a car, you could also turn on your blinker but then go straight. If they do the same, you've confirmed the tail."

"How do I keep an eye on them if they're following me? It's not like I have eyes in the back of my head. And while it might be fun to spin in circles while walking down the street, I'd probably be arrested for public intoxication."

"You always paint the funniest pictures, Cass," Talia says, laughing. "Seriously though...to observe someone following you, use the space around you, such as windows and mirrored reflections, like back windows or mirrors on parked cars. Or, you could act like you forgot something and turn completely around. You'll be able to see their face, and if they will eventually turn too. Be aware that sometimes, the person might follow you side-by-side, such as across the street. In cases like that, use your periphery to see if the person's matching your speed. When you slow down, speed up, or stop, do they do the same?

"If you're driving, try to memorize the vehicle's license plate if you can see it, but at the very least take note of the make/model of their car. If you're walking, look for distinguishing factors: height, build, hair color, eye color, and anyting that stands out, like tattoos or the way they walk. Do they have a limp? The more detail we have, it might help us rule out paparazzi. If it turns out to be one of the paparazzi, then Sebastian and Calder can reiterate the rules of ethics and behavior with them on BLACK Security's terms."

"All good things to know, Talia. Thank you."

Her brow furrows slightly as she leans over to clasp my hand. "Tell me what the person looked like...the one you think has been following you. That'll help us whittle down the list of those who work for the paparazzi. Then we can have you take a look at photos. I'm sure Calder would love to pay him a personal visit."

"That's just it. I never saw his face. I just caught a quick glimpse of a man as he disappeared down an aisle at the library. I can't even tell you if he was heavy set or thin. I do know his hair was short and dark brown. He was about six feet, I guess?" I shrug and shake my head. "Honestly, I only saw him the one time, so he could've just been there at the same time I was."

"But you mentioned that you've felt followed for a couple weeks."

"Now that you said the paparazzi could've been trailing me for a while, who knows how long *that's* been going on. Those guys yesterday did just seem to pop up out of nowhere. Being shadowed by news hounds is probably what I felt, but I'm going to keep everything you've said in mind and pay more attention so I can avoid being surprised by them again. Sorry if I worried you by asking."

"Are you kidding me? Always ask, Cass. It's better to share any worries you have so we can make sure we've got your back too."

"Speaking of asking...I'm hoping you can help." I pause and take a breath. "When I had lunch with Beth yesterday she looked really tired. I know she took on the role of running the Carver family business with her father but, I'm worried she might be more than just run down."

"Oh no...how can I help?"

"Remember how we were going to have Celeste's blood tested for her general health after we determined who her baby's father was?"

Talia's eyes light up. "Oh yeah...that's right. Everything kind of went crazy after we confirmed Phillip was the baby's father. Of course, getting you out of that false arrest took precedent, then stuff started piling up against Phillip once we proved he shot Calder and linked him to the illegal MMA fights. Since they couldn't get him on what he did to Celeste as a teen for lack of evidence, I'm glad that bastard got jail time for her murder."

I fully agree with her sentiment, but to cover my unease with her last comment, I push on. "Did the lab ever give you a report on Celeste's health?"

"I think so." She stands and walks to her desk, then pulls up the case files database on her laptop. "Ah, here it is. I'll print it out."

Handing the paper to me, she tilts her head. "How does this help you feel better about Beth?"

"I'm hoping it'll tell me if Celeste had any of her mother's issues. Her mom died from Lupus complications and my understanding is that Lupus can be hereditary." I stare at the paper, feeling completely lost with all the acronyms and medical jargon with results containing upper and lower ranges. There's a low WBC indicated, and a high erythrocyte (RBC) sedimentation rate listed among other indicators, which may as well be in a foreign language. I don't see any mention of Lupus, but for all I know, it takes more than a blood test to determine that kind of diagnosis.

"Can you make heads or tails of this report?" I ask, flipping the paper around so she can read it.

She shakes her head. "No, but Ben might be able to provide more insight. When you ask him, just tell him that you're going over an old case file for me and need him to help interpret the lab results. It's probably best to keep

Celeste's name out of it. Since his family was close to hers, it might upset him if he knows it's her blood work he's looking at."

I nod my agreement, glad that the lab had registered the blood work analysis under the generic name Patient #1. At least then I won't have to blank out Celeste's name when I ask Ben to explain the results to me. One less lie I'll have to tell. I really hate all this subterfuge, especially because this time around I'm not telling a bunch of half-truths to Celeste's friends and family, but to my own. My intentions might be honorable, but this truly sucks.

"Thanks, Talia," I say, standing. "I'm off to ask for Ben's expert opinion before heading to lunch with Beth."

"You're welcome, but you'll have to wait until he gets here after his shift is over at the hospital."

"Oh." I sigh. "Do you know when that'll be?"

"He's not coming in until after four. He said he had a meeting afterward."

Ugh, I'd really hoped to know for sure before I went over to Beth's house. "Okay, I'll leave him a note."

After I write a note asking for Ben to help me interpret the lab results, I leave it on top of the report on his desk. Breathing a small sigh of relief that Calder's in a closed-door meeting, I head off to steal a small fortune from the Carvers.

BETH ANSWERS the door with red eyes and I instantly walk in and wrap my arms around her. "I'm so sorry," I say quietly, hugging her close. Their main house manager, Beatrice, is standing near Beth's father's office with a worried expression, but I silently wave her away her while patting Beth's back so she knows I've got this.

Sniffling, Beth tries her best to smile as she clasps my hand and tugs me into the foyer. "I'm such a terrible host. Come on. Our lunch is all set up."

I follow her into the dining room and the delicious smell of Vicci's lasagna makes my stomach growl, but as hungry as I am, I wait for Beth to sit first, then take my seat next to her.

"This smells so good," I say, inhaling deeply. When I pick up my fork, but see that she hasn't touched hers and instead is staring at me sadly, I pause. "Is everything okay?"

Beth props her chin in her hand and smiles. "Please eat. Everything is fine. I hope you don't mind if I seem to be staring more than usual, but...it's been so long since Celeste sat here and ate with me, that I'm having a nostalgic moment."

I hold the fork tight and tamp down my guilt. "Stare all you want, Beth. Why don't you tell me a story about your sister. I'll be happy to listen."

She smiles and sniffs back her tears. "You're truly awesome to indulge me." Picking up her fork, she stabs it into her salad. "Let's see. What about the time Celeste got a pony but refused to let me ride it?"

I pause between bites and swallow. "Did she really do that?"

"Yep, sure did." Her eyes light up as she snickers. "I've never laughed so hard when the pony tossed her on the ground and came running over to me." Winking, she grins. "I may or may not have had an apple in my hand."

I shake my head, offering a half smile. "Seems you learned to deal with your sister very well over the years."

"That I did, Miss Cass," she says, pointing her fork at me.

She tells more stories and I respond with laughter or righteous anger as needed while we eat. With each new tale, I can see the love and loyalty Beth had for her sister, even for those times she knew Celeste didn't deserve it.

It's like now that Beth knows the truth about her sister's tragic past, she's able to look past the things that annoyed her as the younger sibling always in the shadow of her sister, to only see the good in Celeste.

Once she's exhausted all her stories, Beth sighs and says quietly, "I wish I could've told her that I forgive her for pushing me away." Despite her suddenly somber comment, her cheeks have a rosy bloom they didn't have before as she digs into her tiramisu.

While I eat my desert, I watch my friend, thankful the tears are gone. Maybe Beth *could* keep Celeste's secret. It would mean so much to her to know she hasn't lost both her mother and her sister. The more I think about it, the more I convince myself that telling Beth the truth about Celeste could solve so many problems. But I could only do so if I knew Beth would keep her sister's secret. Then she could be the one to bring the money to Celeste directly. She'd have to ditch her bodyguard and make sure no one follows her, but she's been adept at that for a while now. She'd have to understand that she'd never be able to reveal her sister is alive. Not even to her father.

The question is...could Beth forgive Celeste for *this* transgression?

I bite my lip, trying to decide how to broach the subject, when it hits me: I'll ask her opinion on that recent story in the news about the teen who set up his own kidnapping in order to extort money from his workaholic parents. Only his plans were thwarted when the police discovered him trying to skip town with the ransom money they'd provided for the kidnappers. *Do you think his family should forgive him?* How Beth responds to that question will hopefully help me decide if she can handle the truth.

I start to ask her thoughts on the story, when Beth puts her hand on her forehead. "I'm sorry, Cass. I suddenly don't feel very well. Would you mind helping me upstairs?"

"Of course," I say, quickly rising to come to her side. "Would you like me to call for Beatrice?

Beth shakes her head, her long, light-brown hair swaying as she folds her arm around my shoulders. "No, if you could just get me to my mother's room, I'll just lay down for a bit."

"Your mother's room?" I grab her phone from the table, then move with her into the hall.

Beth shivers as we start up the stairs. "Mom always had the softest bed."

Once I help her into bed and pull the covers up over her, I touch her forehead, worry starting to creep in. I'm so glad I asked Ben to interpret those lab results. If it seems likely that Celeste was unwell, I'm going to push Beth to be tested. At least then she can get the medical help she needs early on instead of needlessly suffering. "You do feel a little warm. I hope you're not coming down with something."

"Ugh, just what I need. A summer cold. And I've got back-to-back meetings tomorrow."

"Not if you're feeling like this, you aren't. If your father can't make it back in time to take over for you, then have your administrative assistant reschedule."

Her eyes widen. "I can't do that."

"Why not?" I shrug. "That's the great thing about being the boss. You call the shots."

Exhaling a tired sigh, she holds her hand out. "Can you give me my phone?"

When I hand it to her, Beth shivers as she lifts the phone. "Ugh, yeah...I'm not going anywhere like this any time soon."

"Do you want me to stay? Or should I have Beatrice call a doctor for you?"

She shakes her head. "Thank you for offering to stay, but I'll be fine. I'll call her if I need anything. I'm just sorry I had to cut lunch short. One of these days we're going to spend more than an hour together, I swear."

"Promise?" I tease.

"Yeah, maybe a girls night out even."

"Now you're just getting all crazy."

Beth laughs, then winces. "Um, maybe on your way out, could you ask Beatrice to bring me up some Ibuprofen?"

"Absolutely," I say, nodding. "Get some rest and call me when you feel better."

As I start to walk out, Beth calls quietly, "Cass?"

"Yeah?"

"Thanks for coming today, for listening to me ramble, and generally being a very good friend. You've always been there when I've needed you. And since my sister isn't here to do so, I'm thanking you on her behalf too. I'm not sure if I ever did that before, but you went above and beyond for her during that whole switch ordeal. Thank you for being so selfless."

I smile to cover the churning in my stomach. I hate deceiving her, but even if I had told her, Beth's in no shape to help and Celeste's deadline hasn't changed. "Of course, Beth. That's what friends do for each other. Now close your eyes and try to rest. I'll send Beatrice up on my way out."

The house manager is hovering at the bottom of the stairs, a concerned look on her face. "I came to check if you needed anything else for lunch and saw you walking her upstairs. Is everything alright with Beth?"

I shake my head. "She's not feeling well. I put her in her mom's room. She asked for you to bring her some Ibuprofen. And maybe also bring up a heating pad or hot water bottle. She's got the chills. Don't worry about seeing me out. I'm just going to grab my purse and use the restroom before I leave."

"Okay, thank you, Cass. I'm going to take care of Beth right away."

I wait until she heads for the kitchen, then retrieve my oversized purse from my chair in the dining room and make my way toward the bathroom. But instead of using it, I veer toward the elevator at the end of the hall and hit the down button.

My heart pounds against my chest while the quiet elevator moves slowly down to the wine cellar. I check my watch the moment the doors slide open. I've probably got seven minutes max to find the money, stuff it in my purse, and slip out without being noticed.

Just as I step off the elevator and start to enter into the cellar area, I look up and see the camera. *Well crap!* They must've added it since I was here last. As I stare at the equipment, I realize that it's set up to focus on the most expensive bottles in their collection and not the area I'll be in.

A fine sheen of sweat coats my skin in the cool cellar as I remove the four wine bottles and lift up the drawer's fake bottom. My eyes bug at the amount of neatly strapped ten-thousand dollar stacks of hundred dollar bills. *Holy shit! Will I be able to fit all this in my purse?*

Taking a deep breath, I start stacking the money neatly in the bottom in two side-by-side stacks. It takes longer than I thought, because Celeste had actually stowed away a mini fortune.

Three hundred grand weighs more than one would think, I mentally grumble as I lug the heavy purse up onto my shoulder. Or maybe that's just my own duplicity catching up with me. My palm sweats as I fold it tight around the strap on my shoulder, but I move quickly out the front door, determined to leave the Carver estate as calmly but as quickly as possible.

"Miss Rockwell!"

My insides jump and I tense. The deep voice brings

back annoying memories, but I stop and turn just before I reach my car. I'm surprised Marco is still employed by the Carvers considering he was Celeste's bodyguard. "What can I do for you, Marco?"

He folds his arms over his thick chest. "I figured you'd never show your face around here again."

Tightening my fingers around the strap on my shoulder, I can't help but mentally smirk at the bullish man's slightly crooked nose. All compliments of Calder. "I see you haven't changed your asinine attitude," I reply, then turn to open my car door.

"What's in your purse? Looks heavy."

My elbow folds tighter around the leather purse as I pull open my door and face him. "My camera and other equipment. In my real life, I'm a photographer."

His gaze narrows in suspicion. "Open it and let me see."

"That would be a *no*." I stare him down. "Do you really think Beth would tolerate you badgering her guest like this?"

"I don't work for Beth. I work for her father. Now open it," he commands, stepping forward.

"If you so much as lay a hand on me..." I snap. "Not only will I make sure you lose your job, but Calder will *finish* rearranging your face."

Before he can step any closer, I get in my car and shut the door. My whole body coils with tension as I drive away. Marco continues to stare after me with an angry gaze, his hand balled into a fist by his side.

Once I leave the estate, I pull over to a nearby side street and turn off the engine. I was shaking so badly, I could barely keep the car on the road. Taking several deep breaths to keep from throwing up, I force myself to calm down. A few minutes pass before I'm able to hold the steering wheel with steady hands. I glance at my stuffed purse, my stomach still churning, then dig out my phone.

I have the money. I'm bringing it now. I can be there in an hour and a half.

A text quickly pops up.

That's great, but you can't come today. Bring it tomorrow. I'll be out, so use the key. I have a ton of errands I couldn't get done today, because my jerky landlord showed up to fix a plumbing issue he's ignored. He's convinced I won't pay the rent and he'll have to put it on the market soon.

I want to ask her about her baby, but I tamp down the urge. The less I know, the better. Sighing my frustration, I start the engine and head home. I'm so ready for this to be over with. Once I deliver the money, I'll forget I ever heard of Celeste Carver.

CHAPTER TEN

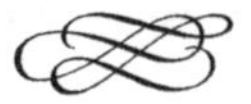

CALDER

While I've got a few minutes between meetings, I walk over to Elijah's office and pop my head in. "You have a minute, Elijah?"

He glances up from his keyboard, dark eyebrows pulled together in intense concentration. "Do I have a choice?"

"Do you want me to sign your paycheck?"

Elijah snaps the laptop closed and laces his fingers behind his head. "What can I do for you?"

I briefly explain what's been happening with Cass's credit card company. "The first time, the thieves bought a bunch of gift cards with her stolen credit card info, making it difficult to trace back to the source. This time around, a new credit card was opened in her name, but the credit card company refused to give her much detail, other than a couple of stores the person hit. I don't trust that they've got the problem fixed. If I give you Cass's card details, can you do me a favor and poke around in the credit card company's system. See what you can come up with. Or any other purchases we might be able to run down. These assholes are messing with Cass's credit and I want it stopped."

"Sure, give me her info and I'll start digging after I get this project done."

Nodding, I look for a pen on his desk. "You don't have a pen?"

He opens his laptop and hovers his fingers over the keys. "I've never needed one. What's the number?"

"I memorized it, but I'll need to write it down to make sure I've remembered it correctly." I pivot and enter Ben's empty office to grab a pen off his desk, but pause when I recognize Cass's handwriting on a note she'd left for him. *What the hell?*

Reading over her note, I look at the lab report underneath and frown. *What's she up to?* She told me she's determined to restart her photography business, so why is she asking Ben to interpret lab results from an old BLACK Security case? And who is the lab report for?

"You coming back?" Elijah calls.

"Yeah, be right there." Grabbing a pen, I walk out of Ben's office.

After I leave Elijah, I stop by Talia's and knock on her

open door. "Hey, Talia. Do you know anything about a lab report Cass asked Ben to interpret for her?"

Talia glances at her watch and says in a low voice, "Is Ben here yet? He should be coming in soon."

I shake my head and step into her office, shutting the door behind me. "What's this about? Who is that report for?"

She shuts her laptop and folds her hands underneath her chin. "Cass is worried about Beth's health. She said she looks exhausted and she's not sure it's all due to taking over as CEO of Carver Enterprises. So she asked me if we ever got the lab results back from Celeste's blood work we had done to prove her baby's paternity. At the time, Cass had also requested to check on her general health status in her blood work as well, since that's the excuse we gave Beth for requesting the sample."

I instantly tense. I hate the idea of Cass inquiring about anything related to Celeste, but since Talia doesn't know Celeste is still alive, I can't bounce my concerns off her. Knowing that Celeste had just tried to get in touch with Cass, but got shut down, I question the reason my fiancée gave for asking about this report. "I see. Looks like I missed Cass stopping by earlier. Where did she go after she left here?"

Talia folds her arms across her laptop. "She planned on meeting Beth for lunch."

"They just had lunch together yesterday." I frown, my suspicious instincts kicking in stronger.

"Apparently that's when Cass noticed how tired Beth looked. She seemed genuinely concerned, Calder. Hopefully Ben can set her mind at ease once he looks over Celeste's results. And, by the way, we're keeping who this blood work belongs to just between us, okay? It might upset Ben if he realizes it's Celeste's."

I shrug. "I'm pretty sure he can handle it, but whatever you think."

When I turn to open the door, Talia says, "I see you and Cass made the paper today."

"Don't get me started." Grunting my annoyance, I face her as she comes around her desk. "The only good thing that came out of that ambush yesterday was that it made sending out an engagement announcement unnecessary."

Talia rolls her eyes. "It's not like you were going to do that anyway, but yeah, I don't think Cass liked being caught by surprise. She asked for ways to know if she's being followed, so I gave her some ideas on detecting a tail and also how to identify them. I told her if she's ever concerned at all, to call us."

"Exactly," I say with a curt nod. "The paparazzi are annoying gnats, always waiting to get right in your face. I'm not sure anyone is truly ready for their dogged craziness, but thanks for giving Cass pointers. I should've prepared her for the onslaught. Her life is about to change as a Blake, but awareness of one's surroundings is incredibly important regardless. At least now, she'll be better prepared when she's out in public."

Talia's phone buzzes and she leans over to grab it from her desk, then turns the screen my way so I can read the text.

Tell Calder to stop socializing and get his ass in here for this meeting.

"Let *Rainbow Master* know I'm coming." I snort. "Can't wait to rib him about that one."

"Gah, do men ever grow out of giving each other a hard time?"

"Are you kidding?" I flash a grin and open the door. "We live for that shit."

On my way to Sebastian's office I send Cass a text.

Your request for Ben to evaluate that blood work better be related to your concern for Beth.

She quickly responds.

I am worried about Beth. We had to cut lunch short because she suddenly didn't feel well.

I'm sure she'll be fine. Ben will get back to you. See you tonight in SoHo.

I'm not coming to your ex's event.

You're coming to support me. Hitting send, I walk into Sebastian's office.

CHAPTER ELEVEN

CASS

I finish up the project I've been working on and put the glue, brushes, and paint away. After getting Calder's last text, I pulled out my supplies to distract myself from the annoyance. Ugh, the nerve of that man. I couldn't believe him insisting that I go to this woman's book celebration under the guise of supporting him? *Pffft* As if!

My phone rings and I quickly pick it up when I see it's an international call.

"Hello?"

"How's my baby girl?" Dad booms. "I got your message and called you the moment we got cell service."

My fingers dig into my phone. "What's going on, Dad? Why are both your house and business phones saying they're disconnected? Did the forwarding company you hired screw up?"

"In case you're wondering, your mom and I are having a great time."

"Uh, I'm sorry. You know I want to know all about your trip, but why are you so calm about this?"

"Well, that's probably because I cancelled the service."

My heart jerks in shock. "But...why would you do that?"

"Because the business kept getting harder and harder to keep up, and your mom suggested it was time for me to retire. I finally agreed. So I sold my business and we put the house on the market, which sold in a matter of days, I might add. So I guess, technically, we're currently homeless."

"What!" My whole body flushes with anger, shock, and sadness. "I loved that Hamptons house, Dad. Why in the world did you sell it? If you needed money...I could've helped pay bills. Why didn't you tell me any of this?"

"Calm down, Cass. I didn't tell you because we wanted to surprise you once we got back."

"I'm surprised all right." I furrow my brow in confusion. "Wait, tell me what?"

"That we're moving to the city to be closer to you, sweetie!" Mom calls out in the background.

My father chuckles. "She's excited about the mother-daughter shopping you two will do—"

"And baby clothes shopping," Mom interrupts. "I can't wait to be a grand-mo-ther," she sing-songs.

"*Mom.* Usually the wedding comes first. You're really jumping the gun."

"Put it on speaker, honey," Mom says in the background. Once Dad does as she asks, her voice comes through louder. "Yes, yes. I know. I'm excited about the wedding too. Speaking of which, have you set a date?"

"We're working on it."

"Well thank goodness for that. Hopefully it'll be after we're settled in our new house in the city."

"Though I'm a bit sad about you selling the house, I'm glad you're going to be closer," I say, my stomach twisting. Mom sounds so excited about being a grandmother. "At least now Dad can have all that downtime he deserves. Are you having a great time on your trip?"

"We're having a wonderful time," they both say, making me smile.

"How about an October wedding, Cass? On the eleventh, maybe?" Mom says, sounding wistful.

Sophie's birthday. How I wish my sister could be here to tell me all my worries about the future are silly. Sadness and nostalgia well up, making it hard to speak for a second. Before I can reply, the doorbell rings. "Oh, someone's at the door. I've got to go, Mom and Dad. Keep in touch and let me know how it's going."

"Will do. Love you, baby girl."

"Love you, dear."

"Love you both," I say as I walk toward the front door.

Hanging up, I peer outside, then open the door. "Hey, Ben. Don't you look nice. What's the occasion?"

He glances down at his charcoal-gray suit and blue tie, then slides his hands in his pockets. "I had a meeting with the hospital board to give them an update on my program for the Vets." He smiles and rocks on his dress shoe heels. "I'm happy to report they're pleased and have approved another year."

"That's fantastic! Congratulations."

He nods and grins. "Though I appreciate the congrats, I didn't drive out here for that." Pulling a piece of paper from his pocket, he holds it up. "I wanted to talk to you about this lab report."

"Come in." As he steps inside, I wave toward the paint paraphernalia near the kitchen. "You'll have to excuse the place. We've been renovating. Thank goodness it's almost done."

"Where's Calder?"

"He has an event to attend tonight," I say, gesturing for him to follow me.

"That's right. Saw something in the news about it.

Why aren't you going?" He follows me to the kitchen and sets the paper down on the counter.

"It's a commitment he made, so he has to show up for it." I shrug, then point to the paper. "You didn't have to come all the way out here to tell me about the report though. You could've just called."

Ben shakes his head, his dark eyebrows pulling together. "This seemed important to you, so I wanted to give you an answer in person." Pointing to the data, he says, "Whomever this person is, she's got some health problems."

I raise my eyebrows. "How do you know it's a she?"

"A guess. I had a fifty-fifty shot." He smirks and points to the left side of the page. "Her white blood cell count is low, indicating a possible autoimmune disease." His finger slides to another section. "And here, this erythrocyte sedimentation rate indicates an infection, possible inflammatory condition, or in an extreme case, cancer. Many more tests would need to be run to determine exactly what kind of issues this woman has."

"So you can't give any type of diagnosis from the data that's provided here?" I ask, trying to keep my frustration at the lack of information from my voice.

His brow furrows. "Is there a particular diagnosis you were expecting?"

"I don't know. You mentioned autoimmune, so possibly something like Lupus?"

"If they had run an ANA—antinuclear antibody—test, a positive result could lean toward Lupus. I'd like to spend a bit more time looking over it and conferring with a colleague. Do you know who this is, Cass?" Ben asks, picking up the paper.

"I was just genuinely curious," I answer his question without actually answering it and shrug. "Okay, that would be great. Thanks for the insight. I'm going to ask Talia how she interpreted the report and if she ever learned what the actual diagnosis was."

He eyes me for a second, then nods. "Let me know once you talk to her. I'll be sure to convey what my colleague says."

My phone buzzes several times in a row with alerts from the new social media app I installed. A couple of big name bloggers have started a live stream from Alana's event and one of their posts stands out. I narrow my gaze on the picture of Calder standing next to a beaming Alana and the headline below it.

"Calder Blake attends Alana's event sans fiancée. Are the 'trouble in paradise' rumors true?"

Someone immediately comments on the blogger's post.

Alana's single. Maybe he's rekindling an old flame!

Ben looks at my screen and frowns. "Didn't the paper say that Calder used to date her?"

"Controversy always attracts more followers."

Pressing my lips together, I watch the gossip thread grow like weeds, then look up to see Ben watching me with sympathy in his gaze. "Can you do me one more favor?"

He flashes a grin. "Anything for my ex-fiancée."

"You can't *ever* say that in public or it'll be taken as actual fact." I snort and shake my head. "Since you'll be heading into town to go home, can you drop me off in SoHo?"

His smile darkens with devilish intent. "Let's confuse the hell out of these media reporting hacks. I'll escort you into the event."

My gaze widens at the long line waiting outside the club the moment we turn the corner and walk along the cobblestone street in SoHo. According to the article I read on the way over, Alana's publishing team rented out the entire club for two hours for a private book signing where celebrities and industry types had been invited to celebrate her InkArt tattoo book hitting the USA Today list. Later the club would open to the general public for a chance to get Alana's InkArt swag and meet the author herself.

"That's a hell of a line," Ben mumbles.

The vibe around The Climb is buzzing with excitement. While navigating the cobblestones in my mile high heels, I feel suddenly self-conscious, so I absently adjust my slinky black dress's halter style around my neck. With a plunging neckline merging into a v-shaped, silver-beaded appliqué at my waistline, the dress's soft silk clings to my breasts and flows around my thighs with the perfect softness to keep the look chic, yet classy. Still, maybe I should've worn a dress that fell below my knees rather than a couple inches above them.

As I try to smooth down my skirt, I stumble slightly, and Ben instantly clasps my elbow to keep me from face planting on the uneven stonework, concern in his dark gaze. "Are you feeling alright, Cass?"

I nod. "I'm fine, just wondering if this was the best dress for tonight."

"You look gorgeous."

I smile my thanks and exhale my relief when we're almost at the door. "The media must be inside covering the event," I say under my breath, glad it looks like we'll be able to slip in undetected. No one is paying us any attention. The crowd is too busy craning their necks with their cell phones at the ready, hoping to capture any famous people who might enter or leave the club.

Just as we reach the area where two bouncers are standing behind a velvet cord, a blonde in line turns her video camera on us, a curious look on her face. "Hey, look. It's Cass Rockwell." She tilts her head, eyeing Ben. "Who's the mystery guy?"

As dozens of cell phones swivel in our direction, flashing rapidly, Ben mumbles, "The media are always everywhere."

I turn and speak to the tall bouncer with curly dark hair. "I'm Cass Rockwell. I'm on the list."

He nods and the other bouncer opens the velvet rope, but puts a hand on Ben's chest as he tries to follow me through. "Her name's the only one on the list," he rumbles.

"I'm her security guard. She doesn't go anywhere without me," Ben says in a stern tone.

The guy starts to argue, but Ben pulls a BLACK Security business card from his suit pocket and hands it to him. "Let me pass or she can't enter."

I nod to the security guy to let Ben follow me in, then whisper to Ben right before we walk inside, "Who knew that Doctor Ben could be so badass?"

"I have many layers you've never seen, Cass." With that cryptic comment, he clasps my elbow and escorts me inside.

When we first walk in, I scan the crowd and instantly recognize a few of my model clients among the guests. Tonight would've been a good night to network if I wasn't so wound up, but I'm only here for one person. I scan for Calder and instantly notice Alana in a fitted floor length red dress with a thigh-high slit as she steps on a raised stage on the right side of the room with a microphone in her hand.

It's not like I can miss her with a zoomed in image of her being shown on two massive screens in either corner of the room. Her dark hair almost brushes her shoulders and is parted in the middle, making her kohl-rimmed eyes look massive above bold red pouty lips. The place is packed and many ladies are hooting and whistling as Alana glances around the room, waiting for silence before she says into the mic, "Are you having a good time?"

Apparently we'd arrived well after the original book signing fanfare and were now entering the party stage.

The moment they all yell, "Yes!" she grins and nods. "I know what you've been waiting for."

"Tell us."

"Dying to know."

"Yes, please!" a lady calls out.

"Simmer down," Alana laughs softly. "Ladies and gentlemen, I give you...Calder Blake."

Right before she says his name, her gaze scans upward, but I don't follow her line of sight because Calder steps onto the stage. The crowd goes wild while Alana hugs Calder, then hooks her arm with his and turns to present him to the audience. Her fawning over Calder infuriates me. The last thing I want to see is him enjoying it, so instead of watching them, I take in the two-story club.

An ironwork ladder centerpiece twists its way from the bottom floor up to the second story, where current partygoers upstairs lean over wrought iron railings to view the entire bottom floor events below. Both floors are alive with people chatting and drinking and colorful spotlights strobe to the music that has started to thump through the speakers.

Along each wall, every few feet, swaths of rich purple fabric flow down the decorative metal columns to the floor. Different collages of colorful tattooed images from Alana's book decorate each of the purple columns, but it's the five foot, black-and-white photo of Calder's muscular back, with his shoulder to hip MMA "Steel persona" skull and raven tattoo, posted at the top of every single purple column that snags my attention. No matter where I turn in the room, he's on display.

From an artist's perspective, Alana was smart to choose a black and white of Calder's back. The absence of color against the rich royal purple background makes his muscle definition and the black ink really stand out. But from a fiancée's perspective, I want to grab that flirty bitch by her silky hair and yank it super-fucking hard.

"I thought he was giving a speech, but apparently this evening is just as much about celebrating Calder Blake's back."

I snort, appreciating Ben's sarcasm as a group of ladies

near us snap pictures of the closest massive poster and gossip amongst themselves.

"I wondered if it might be Calder Blake. My girlfriend and I placed bets on it, but no one could confirm."

"He's hot as fuck underneath that well-tailored suit."

"I didn't know it was him. A Blake? I'm truly and pleasantly shocked."

The more they talk, I wish I hadn't eavesdropped. I talk to Ben so I don't have to listen. "Calder told me that Alana included an image of his back in the book, but not his name. He knew people would try to guess who the model was, but they'd never know for sure, so this reveal baffles me," I say over the music. *It also makes me feel very left out of the loop. How did Alana change his mind?*

"At least we know why there's so much interest about the event," Ben muses as he steps close to show me a promo flyer he'd picked up from a nearby café table.

Find out who the mystery man is from InkArt's centerfold tonight!

Calder was the centerfold of her book? Ugh, I'm really not liking this at all.

Ben nods to the group of professional friends, colleagues, and reporters converging on Alana and Calder as they step off the stage and into the crowd. "If the general public didn't know about Calder's involvement in that illegal MMA ring takedown, they will once the reporters make the connection between that raven and skull tattoo and his Steel persona. It'll be all over tomorrow's newspapers and tabloids."

Why would Calder risk all this exposure? "I think I need a drink," I say, sighing.

"I'll get you something." Ben leans in, his hand touching my back. "What would you like?"

"Whiskey, neat."

His eyebrows shoot up as he straightens. "Are you sure you want something that strong?"

"Yep, it's that kind of night."

"Okay, then." As he walks away, my gaze returns to the crowd that has swallowed up Calder and Alana. I'm annoyed that I can no longer see them, so I step forward and watch with growing irritation once I spy Alana holding court with everyone *oohing* and *aahing* over the book and her talented brilliance of Calder's tattoo.

I want to walk up and smack that book out of her hand. Who the hell does she think she is, exploiting the man I love and his family's name, all to sell more books? And why did Calder allow this? I dig my nails into my palms to calm myself down, but the longer I stand there, the angrier I get. At both of them. As Alana moves closer, signing people's InkArt books and swag along the way, I have to get out of the general area or I just might cause a scene.

The music amps higher as I follow along the wall, heading toward the back of the club. The bathroom has to be back there somewhere. At least there I can splash some cold water on my face and talk myself out of doing anything "rash" as Talia would say. I kind of miss our college days, when my best friend's level head kept me from getting into far more trouble than I could have.

I glance up at the column of purple fabric holding Calder in all his glory just above me. As I pass by it, my annoyed smirk on full display, someone grabs my arm and pulls me behind the heavy cloth so fast that I completely disappear from view.

CHAPTER TWELVE

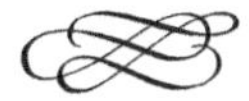

CASS

Whatever my attacker says is drowned by the booming music, but I don't give a damn. Swinging my free hand, I cuff him on the ear. This asshole will rue the day he touched me. "Let go!" He grunts in pain and clamps a tight arm around me, then hauls me through a door behind him and shuts us in complete darkness.

My heart thudding, I scream for help and pound my fist on his chest, then kick the hell out of his shin.

Just when I swing my fist for his groin, he blocks my hit and growls, "It's me, Cass!"

"Calder?" I freeze and blink in the semi-darkness when a low, motion-activated light pops on above our heads. Apparently he'd pulled me into someone's office.

"You scared the crap out of me!" I say, pushing him away. "What is wrong with you?"

"Wrong with me?" He steps back into my personal space, scowling. "Why the hell is Ben all over you? For that matter, why is he even here?"

"All over me?" I run my thumb along his jaw and narrow my gaze at the red lipstick smudge on my skin. "Watch it, Calder. Your hypocrisy is showing."

He captures my hand before I can lower it and yanks me forward, his voice lethal. "You belong to me!"

I'm so pissed and jealous, I don't care if I provoke him. "Do I? Because last night you wouldn't fuc—"

Calder's mouth cuts me off, his fingers digging into my hair, cupping my head tight for his dominant kiss.

I still hate that he let Alana exploit him, but I can't help but respond to the possessive thrust of his tongue tangling with mine. I tug against his lapels to keep him close, moaning against his mouth.

"Fucking hell, Cass. You drive me crazy." He exhales a rumble of frustration and bites the curve of my jaw as he cups my ass and pulls me fully against his erection.

Calder at his rawest is my aphrodisiac. This is the man I fell in love with. The one who doesn't hold back and who demands the same. When he's like this, I always feel like I'm the only one for him. I was too panicked to recognize his arousing aftershave when he first pulled me behind the curtain, but now, as he presses a hot kiss on the skin he just bit, I inhale deeply, enjoying his woodsy sandalwood smell. Calder freezes and his nostrils flare when his gaze locks on the diamond raven choker around my neck.

My eyebrows lift. "Who do you think I wore this for?"

His voice deepens. "It looks so fucking hot on you. I wish you'd wear it all the time. The choker, combined with this dress...you're a walking wet dream."

He's seducing me with just words, damn him. "It's only meant to be worn for special occasions, like...you know, attending an event my fiancé's ex planned that's clearly really all about him." I push up on my toes until our lips are almost touching and wrap my arms around his neck, my tone suddenly serious. "*You* belong to me! And if I drive you crazy, then you'd better do something about that."

He presses his forehead against mine, his breath sawing deeply as he palms my hips, locking us together. "I want you so goddamn bad right now."

I slide my hands into his hair and when I tug on the short strands, his fingers flex against my body. The barely-leashed tension in his hold sends chills of excitement scattering along my skin. I hate that he's holding back. I need him to lose it. To show as much emotion as I feel every time he touches me. My lips shift close to his ear. "I'm not wearing anything underneath this silk dress."

Calder's hands suddenly cinch around my waist and a

low, feral snarl vibrates against my chest. "You came with Hemming like this?"

I grip his shoulders, my fingers digging into his muscles and crushing his suit jacket. "There's only one person I came for."

Heated emotion smolders in his gaze, then his thumbs move to hook the deep vee neckline at my waist and slowly begins to slide upward. With each tantalizing inch of his fingers moving along my ribs, the soft fabric pulls apart. The erotic rub of the silk sliding over my nipples jacks my heart rate and curls my toes in my shoes, but it's the primal desire in Calder's gaze as he exposes my breasts that robs my ability to breathe and turns my legs to jelly. If he weren't holding me, I most certainly wouldn't be standing right now. Swallowing to remain calm, I'm surprised by the huskiness in my voice. "You're still holding back and that's the last thing either of us wants."

I gasp when he suddenly lifts me off the ground like I weigh nothing and his warm mouth latches onto my breast. Tucking my body against his, he nips at my nipple and grabs my bare ass with a savage hold. I'll probably have handprint bruises on my rear, but I'm so turned on I fist my fingers in his hair, wrap my legs around his trim waist, and yank him closer, mewling my pleasure.

Calder walks us deeper into the room and we fall together onto the leather couch. I kick my shoes off as his hands move all over me, scalding my skin with feverish intensity. "Fuck, I can't stop," he growls and slides me fully under him, his tongue plundering my mouth with deep, aggressive I'm-going-to-drill-you-into-this-couch intent.

I kiss him back with just as much fervor, not giving a damn that I'm begging. "Please, Calder." I'm aching to feel him inside me. I tear at his belt buckle and free the button, my movements frantic.

He freezes and puts his hand on the couch, pushing slightly off of me. "Cass, we're supposed to—"

Yanking his zipper down, I grasp his erection jutting against his boxers. "Don't you dare stop!"

He shudders and groans as I slide his cock free, but he grabs my wrist before I can touch him, his voice harsh. "No—" Cutting himself off, he closes his eyes for a second. When they open, the look of dark lust glittering in his gaze makes my stomach clench. "I'm so jacked right now, I might hurt you."

"I'm fine," I say, taking his hand and pressing his fingers against me.

He exhales harshly as he dips two fingers inside me, then buries them deep. "I love everything about you." Withdrawing his hand, he sucks his fingers clean, carnal hunger shining in his eyes. "Every wet, sweet, tasty drop."

Meeting his gaze with equal desire, I roll my hips. "No more waiting."

"Be still, Raven mine." His hand slips into my hair as he lowers himself against me.

I pant hard and tilt my pelvis, giving him better access. Anything to stop the throbbing torture.

Calder rumbles his satisfaction as we connect, then thrusts deep with a low guttural roar of sheer pleasure.

I bite back the pinch of discomfort and instantly move my hips to allow my body to adjust to his girth. Calder counters my movements, his warm lips pressing against my throat. "Fuck, this never gets old, angel. You feel so damn good. I wish I could stay here all night."

"Promise?" I whisper and press even closer, lifting us both off the couch.

He moans and grips my ass cheek even tighter. "You're going to be the death of me."

Rocking against him, my breathing ramps. "Only if you can't keep up."

His hold on my hair tightens and an arrogant purr sounds in my ear. "Let's just see who can keep up."

I get lost in the moment when he pushes his hips forward and rocks hard against me, hitting my g-spot with masterful precision. My orgasm explodes and shudders cascade throughout my body, making my eyes flutter and my toes dig into the sofa.

Still riding high from the pleasure, I push my toes against his pants and underwear, shoving them past his muscular thighs. Digging my nails into his back, I pant in his ear, "I want every part of you touching me, Calder. Don't hold back. Fuck me with all you've got."

He nips at my jaw, then my neck before he withdraws and burrows fully against me. I scratch his back, encouraging his erotic roughness. The sensation of his balls hitting me each time he slams deep, combined with a primalness I've never seen in him before, only heightens my own response. The couch rocks with our movements and bits of something scatter all around us just as my climax shatters me from head to toe. Calder presses his mouth to mine, capturing my scream of ecstasy right before his own orgasm rips through him in a low, fierce roar of release.

My eyes flutter open and the sight of a puzzle piece stuck on its side in Calder's hair makes me laugh. Blowing off a puzzle piece that had landed on my breast, I smirk as I read the label on the container above. "If that's not a big hint that you've totally solved me, I don't know what is."

Calder takes in the colorful puzzle pieces scattered around us and on the floor, then glances up at the empty container lying on its side on the glass shelf above and reads the label. "Solving the Greatest Mystery." Chuckling, he presses a soft kiss to my lips. "As your Master Puzzler, failure was never an option."

We share a smile and then Calder turns his head, listening. "The music has stopped." Pulling back, he stands and fixes his clothes, then grabs a couple tissues from the desk. He leans close and just when I think he's going to kiss me again, he cleans me up, his movements quick and efficient. "We need to move."

Confused by his sudden change in demeanor, I wonder if he knows the music stopping means someone will be entering the office soon, so I stand and step into my shoes while quickly adjusting my dress. Running shaking fingers through my mussed hair, I glance his way. "What's going on? Is someone coming?"

Calder touches my chin, then clasps my hand and opens the door. "Come on."

I have no choice but to follow, because he doesn't release my hand as he closes the door. No one notices us emerge from behind the curtain. The club is packed wall-to-wall now. They must've opened the doors to the outside crowd, but everyone's attention is focused on the stage and Alana, who's standing up in the spotlight, speaking into the microphone.

"Calder Blake? Get back up here." She lifts her hand to her forehead to block the spotlight and peers into the crowd. "I'm sure you all want to hear the inspiration behind Calder's sexy tattoo." Waving her hands, she urges the crowd's participation. "Am I right?"

"Hell yeah!"

"We want to know."

"Give us more."

Several women whistle and cheer, "He's right here,"

as Calder walks through the crowd with determined strides. Once we get close to the stage, I try to dig my heels in and pull free of his hold, but his fingers lace with mine and he tugs me right up onto the stage with him.

"Good evening, everyone," he says, his voice booming. When Alana tries to hand him the mic, he shakes his head. "Can you all hear me okay?" Once the crowd calls out their agreement, he nods and waits for them to settle.

The room quiets and he lifts his hand toward the posters all around the room. "As you know, my photo was listed in the temporary tattoo section in Alana's book..."

As a wave of disappointment buzzes across the room, he shakes his head, a slight grin on his face. "The skull underneath the raven's wing was related to a case I was working on, but..." He pauses and glances my way. "The inspiration for the raven across my shoulders and the reason it's permanently inked on my skin today is standing right next to me. Everyone, meet the woman I can't get to marry me fast enough, my fiancée, Cass Rockwell."

The whole room claps and whoops, and while I stare in shock at Calder, he lifts our clasped hands to kiss my diamond. Smiling widely, he waits for the crowd's *awwwww* to die off. "I know a few of you here tonight are familiar with my talented fiancée, but for those who aren't...in truth you've actually enjoyed her work, and probably didn't even know it."

As he speaks, my heart races when six of my past

clients walk up onto the stage and stand to my right, their glamorous presence creating an excited stir in the audience, along with a flurry of camera flashes. Hailing from five different countries, the four gorgeous ladies and two handsome men are some of the most sought after models in the world. *How did Calder do this?* More than a bit nervous, I smile and nod my appreciation of their support, even though I have no idea what's going on.

Squeezing Calder's hand, I look at him in confusion.

"Every good story brings its symbolism full circle, right?" Calder faces the audience once more, his deep baritone demanding their rapt attention. "I promise, it'll all come together," he says with a softer tone, making the crowd lean-in a little and smile right along with him.

Who knew he was such a great storyteller? My cheeks turn hot when I realize he's now looking at me. "This woman is the most talented, witty, intelligent, and loyal person. She has inspired me in so many ways, just like she's inspired each of you through her work with the ladies and gentlemen standing up here tonight and so many more."

Lifting our clasped hands high, Calder turns our hands over. When the person filming zooms in on my wrist and my raven tattoo shows up on two massive monitors, the crowd goes wild, cheering. "I give you...the anonymous photographer known as Raven. Alana was kind enough to let me share this big announcement and help Cass debut tonight, because she'll be opening up her own photography business right here in Manhattan in the very near future."

"Congratulations, Cass." Alana nods at us as she speaks into the mic. "Everyone here should've received swag bags, and Cass's RAVEN business card featuring appointment only, exclusive shoots, is included in there as well." Sweeping her hand toward us, she beams. "So how was *that* for a great story behind a temporary-to-permanent tattoo?" she asks with a huge grin.

As the crowd applauds and whistles their approval, and reporters and photographers step forward to the bottom of the stage in order to snap photos of us and try to snag interviews with the models, I'm so touched by what Calder has done. The sacrifice he just made, by exposing his role as Steel in a very big and public way, just so he could help me...my chest tightens with emotion.

This whole time up on stage, he never let my hand go, and now with the crowd going crazy, he tugs me to his side and wraps an arm around my waist. To keep from crying, I grip his waist and lean into his strength. All this time, I thought I needed to do everything myself, but there's something so freeing about being with a person who sees you so clearly. Calder heard what was really important to me and he made sure that the identity I'd created and worked so hard to build didn't get lost. "I'm speechless,

Calder. Thank you for thinking of such an amazing way to bring Raven out."

He shakes his head. "I have no doubt you'll make your business work, Cass. I just wanted to remind you that *you* are Raven." Glancing up, he nods to someone behind me. "I believe they're waiting to talk to you."

I barely get a chance to turn around when all six of my past clients converge on me at once.

The curvy Brazilian with luscious hair hugs me and starts talking first. "I'm so glad your sabbatical is over, Raven...er Cass."

I hug her back and smile. "Raven is perfectly fine, but I won't be traveling like I used to—" I say, then get cut off by the two models from Sweden.

"We've missed working with you. What about special projects? We'd love to discuss some with you."

"When will you be available?" the French model, Monique, asks.

"Have you considered helping with our mentoring program? You could shoot amazing portfolios for up and coming models we're working with right here in New York."

"What about a portfolio service where we can keep ours fresh and updated with new concept content?"

My head is exploding with ideas, but I don't know which person to answer first. Calder leans around me and hands them each a gold card featuring a flying raven in the left corner and a new phone number and my email address in black script. "These cards have an exclusive number for past clients only. Don't give it to anyone else without permission. Be sure to send Cass your project ideas, and once she's up and running, she'll get back with you and schedule meetings."

I'm so impressed by Calder's intricate planning, even down to the business cards. I've decided my new phone number will come with a new phone. I'm ready to ditch my increasingly unreliable one. Not to mention, a new number means Celeste can't go back on her word, because she'll have no way of contacting an unlisted number.

After Calder and I thank Alana and leave the stage, he presses a few of the special business cards in my hand. While a swarm of InkArt fans converge around us to get Calder to sign his centerfold picture in their book, my eyes mist over when I realize that the gold card adhered to the black one is actually a fine piece of metal. With the raven and the fancy script stamped out of the golden metal, the whole effect gives the black raven a raised look. It's classy and beautiful, and so *me*. I freaking love it!

I fold the cards protectively in my hand, heartfelt tears trickling down my cheeks. Once the fifty or so people get their books signed and walk away, I push up on my toes to kiss Calder's jaw. "Thank you for believing in me."

He slides his fingers underneath my hair to cup my neck and pulls me close to kiss my temple. "I will always believe in you, Raven mine." Sliding his thumb along the side of my neck, he continues. "Do you want to stay and mingle or do you want to head out?"

I glance around the crowded club as music starts up once more. "I'm ready to go, but I need to tell Ben."

Calder shakes his head. "No need. I saw him leave as I pulled you up on the stage."

"Now I feel bad. I'll have to apologize to him tomorrow."

"Why?" He frowns. "It's not like you were his date."

"No, but he'd gone to get a drink for me earlier." When he shrugs, I sigh. "Never mind. You're not getting it."

Folding his fingers around mine, his frown fades. "I just want to go home and love on my fiancée as hard and as often as she'll let me until we're both completely worn out."

I smile my full agreement, my stomach fluttering in renewed anticipation. Peering through the crowd at the gaggle of paparazzi and other media types hovering just outside the entrance of the club, I grimace. "Do you know if there's a back way out of here?"

CHAPTER THIRTEEN

CASS

My whole body aches as I roll over onto Calder's pillow the next morning. Inhaling his wonderful smell, I moan and slowly stretch my sore limbs. God, he wasn't kidding about going at it hard. I lift my arms and shake my head at the fingerprint bruises on the back of my hands and flex my sore wrists. Calder has to be sporting a few shoulder bite marks and scratches on his back. Grinning like a fool at the memory of last night's adventures, I lift my head when I realize I don't hear Calder in the shower.

"Calder?" I call out, then notice the note he left for me on top of my phone on the nightstand.

Cass,

I didn't want to wake you before I left. I'll be out of the office most of the day on a special project. If you need anything, call Talia or Bash. Will touch base with you later.

Only yours,

Calder

P.S. Last night was fucking epic!

Frustrated that I didn't get to kiss Calder goodbye but that I also missed my chance to tell him about Celeste this morning, I glance at the clock, then scramble out of bed and head straight for the shower. *Ack!* I have less than two hours to get the money to Celeste. She might only be an hour and a half away, but who knows what the traffic will be like along the way.

As I stand in the shower, quickly bathing under the hottest water I can to help massage my sore muscles, I know Calder would insist on going. Granted Celeste was pretty adamant that she didn't want me to bring anyone, but if Calder were here, I'd at least ask him to follow me and wait at the top of the road or something.

Once I get out of the shower and brush the fog off the mirror, the woman staring back at me looks rosy-cheeked and happy. But she also looks a bit tense and ready to get this money delivery over with. "She's also not stupid," I say to myself. Turning, I grab my phone and text Calder the address where I'll be, along with a short note.

I didn't get to tell you about this last night since we got a bit—okay, a LOT—distracted. The address above is where I'm heading this morning to drop something off. Yes, it has to do with the person you didn't want me to talk to, and yes, I promise this is the very last time she'll contact me. I don't have time to wait until you get back. There is a deadline for reasons I'll explain later. Love you!

After I'm dressed, I wrap each of the stacks of cash up in a plastic grocery bag. The doorbell rings just as I set them back inside my oversized purse. Panicking, I quickly grab all the paint supplies I'd bought from the store and drop them over the plastic bags, then snap the middle section of the tote closed.

Surprised to see Ben at the door, I open it with an apologetic expression. "Hi, Ben. I was going to call you today. I wanted to apologize about last night."

He looks confused for a second, then nods. "No worries. I just had a double before heading home. I take it the rest of the evening went well?"

"Yes, it did," I say, smiling. I can tell he's expecting me to ask him to come in, so I keep my hand on the doorknob. "I'm sorry, but whatever this is about, it's going to have to wait. I have an appointment to keep."

A look of frustration flickers across his face "Actually, I really need to talk to you."

"What's this about—?" I start to ask, then cut myself off. "No, I really don't have time. I need to be on the road now."

Ben frowns. "This is important, Cass. Maybe we can discuss while I drive you. Where are you headed?"

I start to shake my head, then glance at my phone in my hand. Calder hasn't responded to my earlier text. I expected an explosive response by now. If I can't have Calder with me today, no matter how he feels about his brother, Calder would expect me to let Ben back me up. He definitely wouldn't want me to go alone. And the look on Ben's face tells me he's not going anywhere. Whatever he has to discuss, it's happening and I don't have time to argue with him.

"If you're up for a road trip, I'm headed to Beacon." I gesture to the tote bag on the counter and make up a feasible story. "I've got this big project planned as a present for Calder, but I don't have the skill set for it. I found a retired lady in Beacon who does excellent work, except I need to bring everything to her by today for her to get it done within the timeframe I need it."

Ben nods and jingles his keys. "Well, let's go then. A road trip it is."

I quickly grab the tote and my phone, then lock up the house before I follow Ben to his car. When he asks for the address, I just give him the street name, town, and zip code. He looks at me expectantly while plugging the info into the GPS. "What's the street number?"

"She didn't give me one. Apparently I'll know her house when I see it," I say, hoping I can convince him to wait down the road while I walk up to her house.

While he shrugs and finishes adding the address info I give him, then starts the engine, I send a quick text to Calder.

No need to worry. Ben just offered to take me. See you tonight.

My phone hangs for a bit before the message sends. Exhaling my relief that it went through, I sigh when I see I only have one bar of service and wait for Ben to tell me why he showed up at my door. He chats about the event the night before and his work with the Vets, but when he doesn't bring up why he stopped by forty minutes into our trip, I adjust the tote bag at my feet to give myself more leg room and finally ask, "What was so important that it couldn't wait for me to pop into the office later?"

"I heard back from my colleague," Ben says, resting his wrist on the steering wheel. "Whoever this person is, she's most likely very sick." He slides his gaze from the highway, dark eyebrows elevated. "How are you feeling?"

Oh shit! He thinks those lab results are mine? I hold my hands up and quickly shake my head. "The blood work isn't mine, Ben."

His brows pull together and his tone sharpens as he grips the steering wheel. "I'm nobody's fool. No more smokescreens, Cass. I know you know, so who does that blood work belong to?"

I glance away, trying to decide exactly what to say. It's probably best to just go with what I told Talia. At least then I'll be consistent. I just hate lying to him.

"It's Celeste's, isn't it?"

I'm so shocked by his comment, I swing my gaze back to him. "How did you know that?"

CHAPTER FOURTEEN

CALDER

I spent the first half of the morning with a real estate agent before unexpectedly heading to the office around ten-thirty. As soon as I enter the main door, I go straight for Talia's office.

Holding her phone to her ear, she beckons me in. "I understand. Thank you for telling me, Ms. Shaw. Yes, I know Adam has a soft spot for her. I'll let Sebastian know."

She hangs up and steps over to the door that connects their offices and opens it. "Hey, can I talk to you for a minute?"

When Sebastian steps through the doorway, I nod to acknowledge him as Talia fills him in. "I just got a call from your father's secretary. She said this is the third day this week that Mina came in late. Your dad told her that Mina's trying to adjust after what happened with Regan."

"That woman is such a busy-body."

When he snorts, Talia rests her hand on his lapel. "She's not tattling, Sebastian. I believe she's genuinely worried about her."

Sebastian presses his mouth together and buttons his suit jacket. "I'll head over to Blake Towers now."

She lowers her hand, her eyebrows lifting. "Would you like me to go? I need to discuss something with Calder first, but I can go after that."

"No, I'll go," he says, shaking his head. "My sister and I haven't talked as much since Joey was born. We should have Mina and Josi over for dinner soon, but for now, I'll take her to an early lunch."

Once Sebastian leaves, I lean against the doorjamb. "Why have I been summoned to your office?"

Tucking her hair behind her ear, Talia says, "The other day when Cass asked me for pointers on how to detect if someone was following her, she mentioned seeing a blur of a dark-haired man."

I stand upright, suddenly tense. Talia holds up her hand and continues in a calm tone. "At the time, I told her it was probably the paparazzi waiting to capture that picture of you two."

"Makes sense. Two of the reporters that day had dark

hair." When she doesn't seem appeased, I frown. "Why do I feel there's a 'but' coming?"

Talia turns her laptop around, pulling up a set of photos. "I didn't want to assume anything, but while I was evaluating these photos Cass took for me over the course of a week, and with Cass's comments stuck in the back of my mind, this is what I noticed."

She selects three different photos and in every one, there's a dark-haired man in the background. Pointing to them, she sighs. "Unfortunately, this is the clearest one, but the face is obscured. In the other two photos, the background image is too blurred for us to determine any facial features. And before you ask, I had Elijah look for cameras around those areas, but the guy seemed to know how to avoid them."

When I pull my phone out to call Cass, Talia says, "This man could very well have been paparazzi. We can't know for sure."

She's clearly tense about something. My gaze narrows. "I know you, Talia. You don't stop digging. What aren't you telling me?"

"I tried to think who might want to follow her. The only person I could think of was Phillip."

I stiffen. "He's in jail. There's not a lot he can do from a cell."

Nodding, she walks over to her copier and grabs a print out. "I agree, but he could have someone else do it for him. Though I'm not sure why he would do that at this point."

I know a reason Phillip might want to follow Cass. I hate that I can't tell Talia about Celeste. My hands curl into fists underneath my crossed arms and I nod to the paper in her hand. "What's that?"

She holds it between her hands. "I have a connection at the prison who provided me with the visitor logs. I asked for the names of people who've visited Phillip to see if I could match their faces to the images we have in the background of Cass's photos."

"And did you find any?" I put my hand out for the paper.

"I'm still working on connecting the names listed with photos once I identify them. But I did see a name that I didn't expect on the list."

She's definitely apprehensive about something. When Talia doesn't hand me the paper right away, I lean over and tug it from her hands. "Who is it?" I ask, while quickly scanning the list. Rage jolts through me when I see Ben's name on the visitor log, not just once, but three times this month.

"What the hell is Hemming doing? He said he hated his father for what he tried to do to Cass...and for what he did to Celeste. For fucking shooting me. That lying son-of-a-bitch! I told you he couldn't be trusted." Crushing the paper in my hand, I turn in the doorway and grit out, "Where is he?"

"He was supposed to come in today, but he's not here yet," she says quietly behind me. "There could be an explanation, Calder. Tread carefully."

"He'll just lie again and give me some bullshit answer," I say in a curt tone. I'm done with giving Ben the benefit of the doubt.

Den moves to stand next to me, his tone calm, but his stance on alert. "Is there a problem, Talia?"

"He's just upset." She puts her hand on my arm. "When Ben gets here, you're going to have a rational conversation. *Right*, Calder?"

I frown, but am saved from responding when Elijah steps out of his office and walks over to us. "I've got a bit of information for you from Cass's credit card company. Apparently this thief wasn't all that smart. Late yesterday, they used the new credit card to set up a bottled water delivery service. Somehow the credit card company didn't catch this one, probably because it's a recurring payment and runs through a different database."

I shake my head. "Is there any way you can get me the idiot's delivery address?"

"I think I might be able to."

"Then do it."

Elijah nods, then furrows his brow. "One thing you

should know. I wasn't the only one poking around in that database."

"What do you mean?" I say, glancing between Talia and Den. "Was the whole credit card company's database compromised?"

"No, that's why I'm mentioning it. The company's database wasn't touched. Only Cass's credit card data has been accessed by someone other than me."

My jaw tightens and I give him a curt nod. "Get me that address." Putting my phone to my ear, I dial Cass's number. "We can pay the asshole a visit later and call the police to arrest him."

Her phone goes straight to voicemail and as I leave the message, "Cass, call me," I hear the buzz of an incoming text in my ear.

I glance down at my phone to read two back-to-back texts from Cass.

My hand tightens on the phone, alarm bells going off in my head. *She's going to Beacon to meet with Celeste and Ben is taking her?* "Fucking hell."

"What's wrong, Calder?"

Why would Cass allow Ben to take her to where Celeste lives? It doesn't make sense. *What if he forced her?* My whole body tenses with the need to hammer Hemming into the ground. "Ben is with Cass. I don't know what his agenda is, but if it involves his father, I'm not waiting around to find out." Bolting for the door, I call over my shoulder, "Have Bash meet me there."

"Where is Cass going?" Talia asks, her tone tense. "Calder. Wait!"

Vibrating with the need to get to Cass ASAP, I stop at the door and glance Talia's way. Cass made me promise never to reveal Celeste's existence, and it's hard as hell not to yell out the truth. This shit is eating me alive.

Setting my jaw, I say, "I'll call you once I'm on the road."

Talia looks at Den who's retrieving his gun from his desk. "Den's going with you. Sebastian will follow as soon as he can." She holds her phone up. "Ben's phone is going straight to voicemail, but Cass's is ringing as if she's out of range. I'll keep trying to get through." As Den walks to the door, Talia's steady gaze holds mine across the room. "I'm not sure what's going on, but you need to give Ben a chance to explai—"

"She is my *life*. If he's done anything to put her in harm's way, I'll roll right over him to protect her," I snarl, then walk out.

CHAPTER FIFTEEN

CASS

I'm tense with the need to know how Ben knew that was Celeste's lab report, so I quickly say, "There was nothing on it to indicate it was Celeste's, so how did you know?"

"Because the lab results also showed a high score for a pregnancy hormone," Ben answers calmly. "The only pregnant person during that time frame, other than Talia, was Celeste."

When I just stare at him while trying to think of what to say, Ben hits the steering wheel with the heel of his hand. "What the hell is it going to take?" Shaking his head, he continues, "I've tried really hard while working two goddamn jobs, but apparently no one in your tight-knit *Blake* circle ever really trusted me. I don't even know why I'm still working there."

"That's not true, Ben." I've never seen him so angry. I feel horrible. He can't leave. "I know that Calder has been tough on you—"

"I would've thought that you of all people would trust me, Cass," he cuts me off, his dark gaze narrowing on me. "But I guess since you're about to marry a Blake, you've already converted to their mindset too. I just don't see the point of sticking around. I mean if I'm never going to be trusted, why bother?"

I touch his arm. "I'm still me, Ben. Nothing has changed. I trust you."

"Really?" He looks doubtful, returning his focus to the road. "What's the big deal then? Why didn't you tell me that I was evaluating Celeste's blood? And for that matter, why are you even looking at a dead woman's blood work?"

The pain in his expression is very real. I imagine that being rejected by his half-brother has a lot to do with his current mood. Or maybe it's because it was Celeste's blood? I bite my lip and try to think of the right thing to say to get him to stay. If he leaves, there's no chance he and Calder will ever become close. Maybe if I share a secret only Calder and I know, that will help Ben feel that he is absolutely trusted. Just like family should be. It's a huge risk, but I believe keeping Ben in our lives is worth it.

I take a deep breath and answer. "Because Celeste isn't actually dead."

"What!" His gaze jerks to mine and we swerve slightly.

"Watch the road," I say quickly, grabbing onto the door handle.

Gripping the steering wheel tighter, he flicks a hard look my way. "Explain, Cass. Right now."

"Before I say anything else, you should know that besides Calder, you are the only other person who knows this. You can't, under any circumstances, tell another soul."

He nods, his tone less combative. "Tell me."

I exhale to calm my nerves. "I didn't have a clue about Celeste's plan until I found the note she left for me on a thumb drive after the trial was over." When he doesn't speak, I relay how she explained what she'd done and why, and how I've had to keep her secret that I'd been duped into helping her carry out ever since.

He doesn't say a word while I talk, but once I'm done, he glances my way with astonished anger simmering in his gaze. "My father told me that he was innocent and I never believed him. He's in jail for a murder he didn't commit and you've had proof this whole time? How can you sit there and tell me that's not some fucked up shit?"

I bristle at his accusation. "I didn't create this mess, Ben. It's not right, I agree, but neither is what Phillip did to Celeste when she was just a teen or throughout her life. Nor the fact that he shot Calder and tried to frame me for

Celeste's disappearance so the blame wouldn't blow back on him. He did everything he could to make sure his past with her wouldn't come out. Your father is a certified psychopath. You know that he absolutely deserves jail time."

His gaze stays locked on the road. "Not for this, he doesn't."

The fact he hasn't looked at me again, worries me. "You can't say *anything*, Ben. Not ever. The digital letter Celeste left behind is destroyed, so the proof is gone. I don't agree with what she did, but there's an innocent child's life to consider in all of this. You know as well as I do, even from prison, Phillip would try to assert his parental rights for a slice of the Carver legacy."

"Is that what makes it easier for you to sleep at night?" he snaps. "Fucked up justice is just that, Cass. Fucked up!"

My stomach churns at his fury. I hated my inadvertent part in this whole deal, but I've learned to live with it. Did I just make a huge mistake by telling Ben?

He glances my way, and his furious expression settles some. "What does any of what you've told me have to do with Celeste's health? And where the hell is she?"

I start to speak when my phone pings with a text from Talia.

Calder is on his way to the address you gave him. I did a bit more digging after discovering a dark-haired man in the background of three of your surveillance photos. To be safe, I checked to see if Phillip had any dark-haired male visitors recently. We're trying to match names to faces now, but one important thing, Ben was on the list of visitors. He saw his father three times this past month. That could mean nothing at all, but I just thought you should know. Can you tell me what's going on? Calder's very tight-lipped, but he's worried for you. Is everything okay?

According to the timestamp of Talia's text, Calder's not far behind us. Maybe ten minutes? I'm so glad for that traffic we got stuck in leaving the city. Calder might be even closer. I quickly text her a response.

Thank you for the update. I had no idea about Ben, but I'm glad Calder's coming. I'm fine right now. We're five minutes away from Beacon.

I text one last note and hit send.

Things could get a bit dicey once we arrive at the house.

Ben glances at my phone. "Your phone works? The service out here is crap so I shut mine off to save the battery."

I stare at my texts stuck in Send mode and my stomach churns. When the undelivered message pops up, I cut my gaze over to Ben. My heart rate jumps as I stare at his dark hair. Not once did I consider that the man following me could be Ben. He's also the right height of the glimpse of the guy I saw in the library. In light of what

Talia just told me about his visits to see his father, I have to wonder if I've been completely wrong about him this whole time. And God, if I was wrong about that, now I've just told him about Celeste...and I'm leading him right to her! I have to do something to stop this.

I bite my lip, then say, "That text was from the lady I'm going to see. She had a family emergency and had to leave. She asked me to come back tomorrow."

"What?" Ben frowns, gesturing to the road. "We're almost there. Did she finally give you her street number? You can just leave the stuff on her porch. I saw plastic bags in your purse. That should keep it safe until she returns."

"Yes, but she said—"

"You said that she needed it today to get your project done in time. Let's just get it delivered."

I take a deep breath and tell myself that it's going to be okay. Celeste needs the money now. I *can't* come back. She said she wouldn't be there today, so she won't see me arrive with someone else and Ben won't see her either. He'll never know this is where she lives unless I tip my hand. "I guess it'll be okay."

Ben looks at me. "You didn't answer my questions. Why did Celeste's health report matter? And where has she been this whole time?"

Now that I'm questioning his motives, I have no problem lying. "I haven't had any contact with Celeste since she disappeared, so I don't know where she is." When he frowns, I say, "The date on that lab report was over a year ago, remember? As for why I asked, I wanted to know if Celeste had developed Lupus so I could convince Beth to get checked. She hasn't looked well lately."

When Ben grunts as if he doesn't like my answer, but at least accepts it, I let out a slow breath and look toward the side road we'll need to take to get to Celeste's house.

While we turn away from the town of Beacon and head in the direction of Mount Beacon, I glance at Ben's GPS, and my heart starts to race all over again. I have less than three miles to come up with a plan to get in and out of Celeste's house without Ben seeing me.

Celeste better not have kid toys on her lawn or anything that would make him suspicious that this house belongs to anyone other than the person I've told him.

As we take the hairpin turn onto the road that'll lead to Celeste's house, I glance down the hill to our left at her ranch style home with a manicured front lawn sitting in the middle of several acres of wooded land. There's no other home around for miles.

"This lady likes her privacy, doesn't she?" Ben mutters and takes the long driveway down from the main road leading to Celeste's house.

"I guess." I scan the well-mowed front and side lawns for any tale-tell signs of Celeste. The backyard isn't massive and it drops off pretty steeply, running right into the woods behind it. There's no car in the driveway, and while I'm relieved not to see any children's toys, my heart twists a little, and I wonder again if something happened to Celeste's child.

Ben parks and takes his seatbelt off. "I'll walk you to the door."

"That's not necessary." Quickly undoing my seatbelt, I slip the tote onto my shoulder and start to open the door, but Ben is already there opening it for me.

With the house key hidden in my palm, I have no choice but to let him walk me to the door. "She said that I should put my stuff under the basket." I squint at the front door. "But I don't see one." Looking at him, I gesture to the side of the house. "Could you check around the back and see if she has one on the back porch?"

"Be right back," Ben says and heads off.

The moment he disappears around the corner, I slip the key into the lock. It takes several seconds that I don't really have to get the key to work, but I finally open the door, then rush toward the kitchen table as fast as I can.

Just like Celeste said it would be, the lockbox is lying open on the table, a few bills next to it. I don't have time to neatly stack the money in it so it'll close. Instead, I quickly pull the two plastic bags out of my tote and set the stacks inside the open box and the door key next to the box.

Ready to get out of here, I take a fast glimpse around

the room and notice that the small house is neat with a couch and side chair in front of a TV. Not a single picture is posted on the walls or any toys are lying about. No photos on the fridge...nothing to identify the owner. I frown at the sparseness of it all. Celeste's life has really changed. Is she happier now? A part of me wants to walk into the bedroom so I can see a baby crib or playpen in there, but do I really want to know for sure? I should just leave and never look back.

Just as I tug my tote bag onto my shoulder, the back door slams open on its hinges and Ben barrels toward me, an angry, determined look on his face.

CHAPTER SIXTEEN

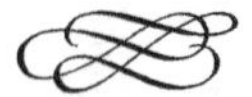

CALDER

The moment I'm on the open road, I gun it, pushing my Charger's eight-cylinder engine to the limit. Gripping the steering wheel tight, I grit my teeth to keep my shit together. I'm going to destroy Ben. Whatever game that two-faced liar is playing, he just lost. You don't fuck with the woman I love.

As the speedometer climbs to ninety and above, Den remains unruffled, his accent smooth as silk. "I sent Talia the address you put in the GPS. You told her you'd call her."

"Not yet," I say in a cold tone. All I can think about is Cass. I'm both angry and worried for her. I know in my gut that she didn't have a choice to help Celeste, because she would've talked to me about it. But fucking hell...I want her to tell me everything. All the time. Not pick and choose. "Why is it so hard for her to let me help?" I finally voice my thoughts. "Why is she so goddamn stubborn?"

Den smirks. "What makes a woman like Cass appealing, besides her free spirit, is her inner strength. She may infuriate you at times, but would you really have it any other way?"

I grudgingly grunt my agreement. He's right, but I don't have to like it. Not in this situation.

"As for Ben—"

"I don't want to discuss that lying bastard." I glance his way, locking a hard gaze with his light-brown one. "And you'd better not get in my way. You're here as back up, not a road block."

My phone rings with an incoming call from Sebastian. I hit the speaker button. "Are you en route?"

"I'll be about ten minutes behind you. Talia said that Ben is with Cass on a trip to this Beacon address and you're worried about Cass's safety? She said you know more. What the hell is going on, Cald?"

Even though every fiber in my being is yelling for me to tell my cousin about Celeste, I honor my promise to Cass. "These are the facts I can say: Cass was worried about Beth's health and she asked Ben to look over Celeste's blood work to see if Celeste had any symptoms similar to her mother's Lupus. Cass didn't tell him that the blood work was Celeste's, because Talia thought it might upset Ben. Ben didn't come to work today like he was supposed to. And now he and Cass are driving to this address in Beacon. I'm worried that Cass didn't go with Ben by choice."

"Talia told me about Ben secretly going to see his father. Tell me about the other?"

"What other?" I ask, frowning.

"You said 'that's all you can talk about.' What's the rest? We are not walking into a potentially volatile situation without all the facts, Cald, so stop fucking holding back."

I lock my jaw. Everything could unravel if I say a word. Before I can speak, Den says, "We'll call you back," and hits the End button.

I glance his way in surprise. "He's just going to call right back."

My phone immediately rings and Den speaks over the ringtone. "Will revealing whatever you're holding back compromise your business partner?"

Pressing my mouth in a tight line as the phone goes silent, I slowly nod. "It could potentially, yes."

When Bash calls back again, Den asks, "Can we still do what needs to be done without this information?"

"We can, but knowing all the facts would make it a hell of a lot easier," I grate out.

Nodding, Den answers the phone to Bash's immediate rant. "Don't you dare hang up on me again or you're fucking fired."

"You do realize I don't need to work, right?"

Bash is probably as shocked as I am, but I give Den props for staying cool under pressure. He looks at me, his brows raised expectantly, so I offer my cousin an answer he'll accept. "Bash, this road trip could be all the motive Ben needs to hurt Cass."

A couple seconds of silence comes across the line. "I hear your engine roaring. Don't get yourself fucking killed, Cald. I'll be there as fast as I can."

Before I can thank him for trusting me, he hangs up. "He's pissed," I mutter.

"He's in. That's all that matters," Den muses. "Where was he anyway?"

"He's worried about Mina," I say, rolling my head from one shoulder to the other to ease the building tension of not being able to get to Cass fast enough. "The fact her best friend Regan ripped off her father's company for millions before disappearing has really shaken her. Bash went over to take her to lunch."

"She needs to be pushed, not coddled."

The Brit's on a roll today. I snort at his bluntness. "She's the only girl in the family. We all look out for her."

"You're doing her a disservice. Mina is quite capable."

"Of course she's capable, but watch what you say to Bash." I glance his way, but he's staring straight ahead, his expression unreadable. "When it comes to Mina, he's very protective of his little sister."

Den flicks me an unapologetic look. "I only say what matters, Calder."

I hold his gaze for a second. "Fair enough, but don't say I didn't warn—"

An incoming call from Elijah interrupts us and I quickly put his call on speaker. "What's up, Elijah?"

"Sending you the address now where the water was delivered."

"That's going to have to wait. I don't have time—"

"Calder," Talia interrupts. "Look at the address."

I look at Den, who pulls it up, then quickly turns his phone my way. When I see it's the same address I plugged into my GPS earlier, I jerk straighter in my seat and snarl, "Fuck this shit! All bets are off. Conference in Bash, Talia, so we're all on the same page."

Once Talia gets Bash on the line, I tell them the rest of the story. "Celeste is actually alive." While Bash mutters, "motherfucker," I tell them all what happened and how we got to where we are today. "This address we're going to is apparently where Celeste is currently living."

"I've been checking up on that address. It was owned by a man for twenty years and he sold it for cash last year. The transaction was through an agency, so I can't confirm who the buyer was. It could've been Celeste," Talia says. "Didn't you say that Cass said she wasn't going to help Celeste when she tried to contact her? Wonder what changed her mind?"

I narrow my gaze on the road, my stomach clenching as my worry deepens. "I don't know, but something convinced her otherwise, and somehow Ben's involved."

"It sounds like Cass was set up, but why?" Bash says.

Talia speaks closer to the phone, her voice suddenly tense. "I still can't get through on her phone. Get to Cass fast, Calder. I think this whole thing might be some kind of trap."

I hang up with them and a few minutes later my muscles tighten as I make the hairpin turn onto the road Celeste's house is on. I can see the small house sitting down a hill on several acres of land that runs parallel to the road. Off in the distance, Ben's car is sitting in the driveway. Just as I push on the gas, the car windows rattle from a horrific boom. Bright light flashes within the house below and it explodes into a ball of fire.

Cass! God, no! Slamming on the brakes, I jam the gear into Park. Since the driveway is on the opposite corner of the property, running a straight line from here will get me there faster, so I jump out and call to Den, "Meet me down there."

It's a steep hill, but I don't remember getting from the top to the blazing inferno below. The smoky fire grows bigger the faster I run. I can only get so close because of the heat.

My heart thunders and my eyes water as I peer into the raging blaze for any signs of life.

Nothing.

The fire is relentless and massive, its flames viciously consuming everything that mattered to me, burning up all my dreams, reducing my heart to ashes.

I stare in shock and my hands shake as I scrub my face in the hopes it's just a nightmare I'll wake up from. But the heat pushes me farther back. I stumble, my legs hardly working.

Sweet Cass. My angel. My life. I swallow several times, but I just can't believe it. My chest feels like it's caving in and I fall to my knees unable to catch my breath.

Den's hand lands on my shoulder and squeezes. I barely feel it. Everything inside me goes numb. My mind shuts down. Coldness seeps into my soul, chasing the heat from my skin.

When a shadow forms to the left of the house in the smoke, I blink. I quickly stand on unsteady legs and stare harder, whispering to Den, "Do you see that?"

The shadow's trying to run, but stumbling. I start running toward the person, yelling, "Cass?"

"Calder? I can't see you." Her croaks are barely heard above the noise of the inferno, but God it's music to my ears. I rush forward into the smoke billowing out of the blown out windows on the side of the house and lift her up into my arms.

Moving away from the smoke and heat of the fire, I set her down in the yard, then skim shaky hands all over her.

From her gorgeous hair, to her shoulders, to the tips of her fingers, I check every beautiful, warm part. "I've never been so scared, Cass! Are you okay?"

As I cup her soot-covered face and press my lips to her forehead, so fucking thankful she's alive, Cass clasps my wrists and coughs a couple of times, then pulls back to meet my gaze. "I—I'm fine. We're fine."

"That was a close call," Ben says quietly behind me.

The sound of his voice sets me off. I don't even bother looking as I pivot and swing with one fluid motion. The pain in my hand is overshadowed by the satisfying *crunch.* But it's not nearly enough.

He stumbles back and covers his bloody nose. "Have you lost your goddamn mind?"

"Calder!" Cass screams and tries to grab my arm.

"You lying sack of shit! I'm going to fucking kill you for putting Cass at risk."

"Liar? What the hell are you talking about?" Ben puts a fist up and beckons with his other hand, yelling, "Come on, asshole! It's way past due."

"Why don't you tell Cass about how you've gone to see your father three times this month? The man you swore you were done with, remember that? What the hell is your end game, Ben? Are you working with your father?" When I snarl and step forward, ready to pummel him into oblivion, Cass jumps onto my back.

Wrapping her arms and legs tight around me, she yells

in my ear, "Stop, Calder! I would be dead if he hadn't grabbed me and run us out of that house. He *saved* me."

I don't want to let go of my anger. The emptiness and terror I felt when I thought I lost her hasn't left me. It's still festering and swirling inside me, needing a release. I advance on Ben, then jolt to a halt when sudden pain radiates from both my ears and my head snaps back. "Ow, Cass!" I quickly reach back and grab her ass, lifting her to relieve my pain.

Releasing her bull-horn hold on my ears, Cass falls against my back once more and squeezes my neck in a tight hug. "Sorry, but you weren't stopping. I had to snap you out of it."

"Was anyone else in the house?" Den looks between Ben and me. Once we shake our heads, he says, "Then if everyone's all right, I suggest we leave the area as soon as possible."

I pull Cass down in front of me and wrap an arm around her. When we don't move right away, Den adds, "Unless you'd like to answer the authorities' questions as to why you're here and if you had anything to do with this inferno? The fire trucks are about three minutes out."

Realizing he's right, we all nod. While Cass retrieves her tote bag, I refuse to let her hand go and I steer her toward my car.

"I'll ride with Ben." Den says, then walks away.

Once Den reaches Ben's car, I meet his gaze across the

driveway. "Text Sebastian and tell him to meet us in the town of Beacon. We passed it on the way here, so he could get there before us. We'll find a place to convene there." Den inclines his head in agreement and climbs in to Ben's car.

CHAPTER SEVENTEEN

CASS

As soon as we're seated in his car, Calder takes my shaky hand and presses his lips to my palm. I don't know why I'm trembling, but the look of love and worry in his eyes slays me. After I quickly clean up my face with a wipe, he takes my hand and sets it on the gearshift, then rests his big hand over mine as he shifts the gear and we follow Ben's car. When his fingers lock with mine around the gear, the warmth of his hand seeps into me, settling my nerves. A few miles pass before my body stops shaking, but my mind is screaming with questions. I know he's waiting for me to talk.

"I still don't know what happened," I say quietly.

Calder rubs his thumb across my engagement ring to let me know he's listening.

I swallow and recount the last few seconds before the

explosion that felt like both an eternity and a movie on fast-forward. "I was standing in the kitchen and Ben kicks in the back door." I close my eyes and shake my head. "I was confused by what he'd done and a bit scared, because he looked angry. Then he ran in, grabbed my hand, and yanked me toward the back door, yelling, "Run, Cass!"

I open my eyes to see Calder watching me. "All I did was react. I trusted his lead and ran. If Ben hadn't tugged me down that steep hill behind the house, where we both pretty much rolled all the way to the bottom, I don't know if I'd be here talking to you right now."

He squeezes my hand and glances toward the road, his voice rough, on edge. "Ben using the hill to get you out of the way quickly saved you both. I've seen more than my share of explosions in my active military days. Beyond flying debris, the concussive force can cause major damage. Why were you even there?" His gaze returns to mine, his eyes darkening. "Did Ben force you to go?"

"No, Ben didn't force me. I told you that he was going with me."

"You sent a text, Cass. After learning that Ben lied about his father, I didn't know what to think. When you told me about Celeste, you said you told her not to contact you again, remember?"

I nod. "Then she sent the book."

"What book?"

"The one you put on our bed. That was the same book

Celeste used to confess what she'd done to Phillip."

"Son of a bitch!" he grumbles, his hand on the steering wheel tightening.

"The note she left for me said that her medical problems were more than she'd planned for and she needed me to get the money she'd hidden away for herself at the Carver estate or she'd get kicked out of her hous—" I gasp and clamp my other hand over my mouth. Fingers trembling, I pull them away from my lips. My breathing increases and I feel a bit dizzy. "Oh God...all that money. I'd just set the stacks on the table. It blew up in the explosion."

"Calm down, Cass. Don't worry." He holds my gaze for a second before returning his to the road. "Celeste knew exactly what she was doing."

His sharp tone surprises me. "You don't understand. It was a *lot* of money. Three hundred thousand. She'll never believe I didn't have anything to do with what just happened—"

"Celeste set you up. You were targeted all along. The fact that she wasn't there when the house blew up is very telling."

"What! You think the house blew up on purpose?" *Ben's reaction now makes more sense. But how did he know?* Looking at Calder, I furrow my brow. "But I checked on Celeste's story. Ben confirmed that her blood work shows she's not well at all. She's very sick."

He gives me a look. "You weren't completely truthful about your reason for asking for that lab report."

"I was trying to do my own investigating first," I say in my defense. "And I did share that I needed to help Celeste. It's not my fault you distracted the hell out of me last night. I told you I'd tell you everything when I got back."

He grunts and returns his gaze to the road. "Celeste's poor health may or may not be true, but this part definitely is: I had Elijah check on your credit card issues in the hopes we could stop it for good. Celeste is the one who opened the latest credit card under your name."

My face flames with fury and I curl my hand into a fist on my lap. "Are you serious? I'm going to cut a bitch!"

Calder nods. "She's probably behind the other credit card issues you had too, which falls in line with what you said about her needing cash for a while. We know for sure she was behind this last credit card, because she screwed up and used that card to order a bottled water delivery service to the same Beacon address."

"I tried to be smart and double-check her story. I knew I'd never be able to look Beth in the eyes again if there was something I could do to help her sister and I didn't. I considered telling Beth, but I don't think she could handle the truth. I believe it would actually destroy her to know Celeste lied to her whole family, so I retrieved the cash and took Ben with me as back up to deliver it. Er...

speaking of Ben. I ended up telling him the truth about Celeste on the way."

Calder sighs, then nods. "Talia, Den, Bash and Elijah now know too. I had to fill them in once we discovered Celeste had been targeting you for a while."

I'm relieved that he didn't ask me what prompted me to tell Ben. The last thing I want is for Calder to encourage Ben's consideration of leaving BLACK Security. Then again, after Calder's punch earlier, my effort to forestall Ben from leaving may be a moot point. I rub my throbbing temples and try to focus on one worry at a time.

"Celeste promised once I delivered the money, this would be the last time she contacted me. I didn't realize she meant because *I'd* be dead. *Why* did she do this? Why did she destroy all that money and a house?" My stomach churns with disappointment in myself for not seeing through Celeste's ruse. As much as I'd like to believe otherwise, tigers really don't change their stripes, and apparently a sick tiger is far more deadly. "I can't believe I fell for her sob story. I feel like such a fool."

"Don't blame yourself. Celeste learned from the best. Phillip was the master manipulator. The question we have to answer now is: What does she gain from trying to kill you?" He pauses, his gaze narrowing on the road ahead. "We have the advantage for now, because she doesn't know that you didn't die in that explosion."

He releases my hand on the gearshift and slides his

thumb down the side of my neck, his steely gaze locking with mine. "This is far from over, angel. No one attacks the woman I love and walks away. Going after a Blake was Celeste's fatal mistake."

Just as we reach the town of Beacon, a text pops up on Calder's phone from Sebastian.

Meet me at Marrows, a restaurant on the west end of town.

We quickly drive through the picturesque town on the edge of the Hudson, then we walk into the quaint restaurant, Marrows. I'm surprised that it's empty. Sebastian is sitting at a big round table in the far corner of the room.

As we follow Ben and Den across the room, Calder clasps my hand and keeps me close.

Once we reach the table, Calder waits for Den and Ben to settle on Sebastian's left, then he pulls me on the other side of the table next to Sebastian before he slides into his seat beside me.

Sebastian raises his eyebrow at Calder, but doesn't comment. Glancing at his watch, he says, "We have one hour to ourselves before the restaurant opens for dinner. Den gave me a summary, but let's debrief on the details of what the hell just happened so we can plan what to do next."

"You first." Calder looks at Ben across the table, who's feeling the bridge of his swollen nose between his thumb and pointer finger. "Start by explaining why you've been visiting your father in prison, a man you profess to despise for what he did."

"I don't owe you any fucking explanation," Ben snaps. "You broke my nose."

"Bill me," Calder says curtly. "My question still stands."

Sebastian looks at Ben as he glares at Calder. "I realize there's tension between you two, but I'm asking as your employer who's had to deal with the fallout your father caused. You visiting your father seems to completely go against what you've said to us."

Ben takes a deep breath, his nose wheezing. "My mother has been sick for a month. She continues to believe in my father's innocence and it stresses her that she hasn't been well enough to go see him. She asked me to go for her. I did, because I love my mother. End of story."

"You could've just said that," Calder says, his tone more subdued.

Ben folds his arms. "Like you would've believed me."

I put my foot on top of Calder's under the table and nod toward Ben. He frowns, then sighs. "I'm sorry I broke your nose." Glancing my way, he runs his knuckles along my cheek. "Thank you for saving Cass. I can never repay you for what you did to keep her safe."

"She's family," Ben simply says, drawing both our

gazes. He smiles at me, nodding when I smile back. "At first I couldn't figure out how Cass got inside, but then when I saw a red light turn on the moment she moved into the room, I noticed the wired black box to the right of the door. Then the red light started to blink. Whatever it was, my gut told me I had very little time to get Cass out." He shrugs. "So I just reacted the best way I knew how."

"Now that we have proof there was a bomb, we need to find her," Den says, pushing his phone to the center of the table.

"Cass and Ben," Talia's voice comes through Den's speakerphone. "I'm so glad you're both all right! I've sent each of your phones the photo of the man I believe may be the person who's been following Cass. Dan Matthews is ex-military, whose special skill was infiltrating computer networks. He's also known as a man-for-hire. He wasn't listed among Phillip's visitor logs. He's too smart for that. He sent a go between, whom I traced to him via their preference for frequenting the same bar. He and his contact person weren't covert enough while staggering their entrances and exits. Thanks to cameras outside the bar, I figured their connection out pretty quickly."

"What do you think he wants with Cass?" Sebastian asks.

"I think Cass is a means to an end," Talia says. "Since Phillip didn't kill Celeste, he knows someone framed him."

Ben nods slowly. "My dad has always maintained that he'd been set up to take the fall."

"Right," Talia continues. "So my guess is, Phillip thinks Cass might know who that could be, hence him hiring Matthews."

"But why now?" Calder's gaze pings to all of us. "Why after all this time has this guy started following Cass?"

"How long has your credit card thing been going on, Cass?" Talia's voice comes closer to the speaker.

I try to think back. "The first time was at your baby shower."

"Ah, okay," Talia says. "It's possible that Cass's credit cards weren't the first place Celeste tried to get money. We have no idea how long her money issues were going on."

"I see where you're going with this." Ben sets his arms on the table, leaning in. "You think Celeste might've tried to use an old credit card or an old account, and my father had people watching the accounts."

"That matches with what Elijah told me," Calder interjects. "He said that someone else was in the credit card company database looking at Cass's information."

"Which means this Matthews bloke might also know about the bottled water delivery address and could already be here." Den rubs his hand on his chin, his brows pulled together in deep thought. "What I find odd is that

Celeste made this kind of misstep. She had everything sorted. She'd done everything right. She didn't contact family. She stayed off the grid. The need for money might've driven her to use Cass's credit to get by, but why did she sign up for a delivery service?"

"That does seem inconsistent with someone trying to stay under the radar," Talia muses. "We may never know why, but that answer doesn't explain how we locate Celeste *now*."

Sebastian looks between Ben and me. "Is there anything you saw in Celeste's house that could give us a clue as to where to look for her?"

I start to shake my head, then jerk my gaze to his. "The medical bills!" Frowning, I continue, "Ugh, but I didn't bother looking at her name."

"Where was the bill from, Cass?" Talia asks.

"I remember a red half heart merged with a white cross, on top of a light-blue shield. It was from a hospital." I squeeze my eyes shut, trying to remember. "Saint—"

"Got it. It's Saint Andrews," Elijah's voice booms through the speaker. "Give me a minute to dive into their system."

"Scan their database for the Beacon address," Talia says in the background. "Then we'll be able to determine what name Celeste used as a patient there."

"She's so good," I whisper to Calder.

Sebastian nods. "She is, but Celeste didn't count on a whole team coming after her. We'll find her."

We all wait in tense silence until Elijah speaks again. "She's going by the name Cassandra Roswell." When I grunt my annoyance, he says, "And we don't have to bother looking any further. She's at the hospital, currently admitted as a patient."

"What's she being treated for, Elijah?" Ben asks.

"I'm scanning the doctor's notes. There are a lot of codes on here. Lupus is mentioned earlier in the notes, then chemotherapy. It looks like she's being treated for kidney issues related to the chemo drugs."

Beth would be so upset to know her sister is going through this alone. My sad thoughts must've shown on my face when I glance Calder's way, because he shakes his head in a fast jerk. "Don't feel sorry for her, Cass. Not one ounce of sympathy. The woman tried to take you out."

"I know." I rub my forehead, my hand shaking. "I can't help but think about Beth."

He wraps an arm around my shoulder and kisses my temple. "Beth has already buried her sister. This guilt you feel, you have to let it go."

I take a deep breath and nod. "So what's the plan now?"

Calder looks at me, his expression determined. "We're going to pay her a surprise visit."

CHAPTER EIGHTEEN

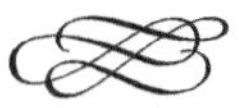

CASS

While Ben, Sebastian, and Den remain in their cars to stay in touch with Elijah and Talia as they try to determine a current location on Phillip's guy, Matthews, Calder and I walk into the hospital to "visit" with Celeste. Even though Sebastian and Den didn't like us going in alone, we all agreed it would look less suspicious if just two people went to see her.

"As much as playing the grieving, vengeful fiancé appeals in order to put the fear of God into Celeste..." Calder reaches for my hand as we get off the elevator on the fourth floor where Celeste is staying. Folding his fingers with mine, he continues, "It's a little too close to home for me, Cass. I imagine Celeste's, 'Oh, shit! I didn't kill her like I thought,' reaction when we walk into her room will yield some telling results before we drill her for the full truth."

"Are we going to call the police after we talk to her?"

He looks at me. "Yes, we will. She has crossed the line."

I agree it's the right thing to do, but I squeeze his hand. "I'm so afraid Phillip will somehow be released from jail once this comes out."

Calder pulls my hand to his lips and presses a kiss to my knuckles. "He will *never* touch you. Not as long as I'm breathing."

"But who's going to protect you?"

His smile is full of confidence. "Family, both the business and personal one."

We reach Celeste's room, just as an older doctor with thinning hair and a curly-haired nurse come from the opposite direction. She smiles to acknowledge us. "Are you here to visit with Miss Boswell?"

When we nod, the doctor stares at me, a look of pleased surprise on his face. "I wasn't aware that Cassandra had a sister."

Ugh, why does her face have to look like mine? I quickly make up an answer. "We um...haven't been super close in the past, but now that she's sick, I think it's time to try to mend fences."

He inclines his head in approval. "I'm Doctor Patterson. I'm glad she'll have someone to talk to. This week will be rough with a battery of tests that will exhaust her. Once I'm finished going over some of her lab results, you're welcome to visit."

The nurse gestures to the waiting area just down the hall. "You can wait there."

We thank her, then walk down the hall to sit in uncomfortable chairs.

"I don't like this," Calder mutters and texts Sebastian an update the moment we sit down. Two seconds later, his phone rings. "Yeah, we're here until the doctor's done."

My phone buzzing in my purse distracts me from the conversation. I retrieve it from the tote and see that it's my doctor's office calling, I can't believe it. *Of all the rotten timing.* With Calder talking in the background, I want to be able to hear, so I walk farther down the hall and answer the call. "Hello?"

"Is this Cassandra Rockwell?"

I glance back at Calder to see his gaze pinging between me and Celeste's room, while his phone is to his ear. "Yes, this is she."

"This is Rachel from Doctor West's office. We're just calling you with your test results."

I exhale quickly. "Yes, please let me know the results."

"Doctor West wanted to call you himself, but he got called into an emergency C-Section, and he knows you've been anxiously waiting an answer. Your AMH level did come back on the low side, but...he wants you to know that that doesn't mean you can't conceive, Miss Rockwell."

My heart sinks and it's hard to take a breath. "I know that means it'll be a lot harder. He explained it to me, but at least now I know."

"The doctor would like for you to come in for a follow up and he'll discuss your fertility options with you. Would you like to make an appointment now?"

I look at Calder, who's off his phone and already headed in my direction. "No, I'll call back later. Thank you for calling."

"Bash said Elijah tapped into as many cameras as he could and he caught the Matthews guy driving out of town in the same direction we did earlier."

"Do you think he's coming here?"

Calder shrugs. "We don't know for certain, but Elijah is now plugged into the hospital's security cameras to be our eyes around the hospital while we're in here." He tucks my hair behind my ear and nods toward my phone. "I could tell that call bothered you. Who was it?"

I glance over his shoulder and once I see the hallway is still empty, I drop my phone in my purse and nod. "I didn't want to say anything to you before now because I wanted confirmation."

Calder takes my hand. "You're shaking, Cass. What's wrong?"

I exhale and try not to let the tears I feel burning behind my eyes fall. "I know we haven't been trying for children, but I couldn't understand why we haven't gotten pregnant considering I haven't been on birth control for months. I wanted to know if I was the problem. That was my doctor. My AMH levels are low. AMH measures the health and quality of my eggs. Low isn't good. It means, it'll be much harder for us to get pregnant."

"It'll happen when it's meant to, Cass."

When Calder cups the back of my head and pulls me close, the tears start to fall anyway. I look up into his handsome face, loving him so much. "I wanted you to know this before you married someone who might not be able to give you children."

He smiles and wraps his arms around me. "I love you, Cass. That's all I care about."

I push back a little. "I want you to have your family, Calder. That's what you said you're ready for, remember? And after everything you've lost, you deserve to have your own children and raise many little hellion Blakes. I won't be the reason that never happens."

He locks his arms around me, refusing to let me pull away. "You're just going to have to trust in us, Cass. And if it doesn't work to have our own, we could consider adoption."

I shake my head. "While I believe adoption can be wonderful, you deserve biological children too. Your own blood, Calder. I don't want to take that opportunity away from you. That way your branch of the Blake family can truly live on and flourish."

"*My* branch is so twisted and full of knots, the Blake part no longer exists anyway," he says in a dry tone.

"I'm serious, Calder." I say, my heart hurting. "I won't be the reason you don't have your own children."

"Are you deciding for me, Cass?" He frowns, his hold on me flexing with tension. "It sounds an awful lot like you are."

"No, that's not it. I—"

"Then what are you saying?"

I look away, my gaze blurring with renewed tears. My heart hurts so much. "I don't want to fail you."

Calder cups my cheek and turns my head until my eyes meet his. "You will never fail me. Not fucking ever. I love you more than life itself, Cass. If it's just the two of us until we're a doddering old couple, I'll still consider myself the luckiest man alive."

He presses his lips to mine and the tenderness makes my heart trip. Pulling back, he meets my gaze. "Whatever future we face, we'll make plans that work for us. We'll do this together."

I let out a relieved breath, tears trickling down my cheeks.

Calder swipes the wetness away with his thumbs, his green gaze searching mine. "Okay, Raven mine?"

I nod, and as we exchange a smile, the nurse we saw earlier walks past us, then pauses and turns back. "Have you seen your sister yet?"

When I shake my head, she smiles. "Then go on in. We finished up a little bit ago. I'm sure she'll enjoy your company."

"Probably less than you think," Calder murmurs as she walks off. Wrapping his arm around my shoulders, we walk together to Celeste's room.

I knock, but when Celeste doesn't call us to come in, I open the door anyway. Calder's right behind me as I step into the room, but then we both exchange a look of alarm. The bed's empty. My heart races as he quickly checks the bathroom. No one.

As I ask, "Where did she go?" he pulls his phone out and makes a call.

"Elijah, start checking every camera from the fourth floor down. Celeste bolted before we could talk to her." Hanging up, he makes another call. "Bash, Celeste is on the run. Elijah's scanning the hospital for her. Stay in touch with him. Between you, Den, and Ben, try to cover all the exits. Cass and I will work our way down. If she gets out of this hospital, we may never find her again."

As soon as he hangs up, his phone rings. Calder closes the room door and puts it on speaker. "Have you found her, Elijah?"

"Not yet, but we've got another problem. Matthews is

here. I just caught him on camera walking into the hospital from a side door."

Calder frowns. "How did he find us? And why did he enter the hospital that way?"

"Give me a minute, let me rewind the video." Calder and I wait while he's typing in the background. "Yep, he walked through the parking lot on that side of the hospital."

"Did he look at or hang around any car in particular?" I ask. "Could he have traced Celeste through the car she's driving?"

"I'll bet that's exactly what he did, Cass." Talia jumps in. "Elijah and I think he got her address from your credit card...and that's how he showed up in the town while you guys where there. Den said he remembers a car like Matthews's driving past him as he pulled Calder's car down the driveway toward the house."

"His hacking skills are as good as mine," Elijah says. "He probably tapped into the local DMV and crossed referenced that Beacon address. Damn, we should've thought of that, but there wasn't a car there. Anyway, my guess is once he saw the house was up in flames, the DMV data gave him everything else he needed, from her car's VIN number to the alias she's living under. All he needed was the VIN number to trace her car's GPS straight to the hospital."

Calder meets my gaze, lines of concern around his

mouth. "Tell us which exit he came through, Talia. We'll head there now. Contact the guys and let them know to drive to that side of the building. Elijah, while Talia watches that exit for any sign of Celeste, can you check the earlier footage to see which car he paid more attention to? Whatever Matthews's agenda is, it can't be good. We need to get to Celeste before he figures out that she's been spooked and then doubles back for her."

By the time Calder and I reach the entrance, we haven't seen any sign of Celeste. We walk outside and the parking lot is quiet. He immediately calls Talia. "Any sign of her?"

"Nothing yet, Calder. She hasn't left the building."

"Matthews focused on a dark-blue sedan," Elijah says. "I'm moving over to the DMV now to get the plate number."

A few seconds pass, then Elijah comes back on the phone. "Got the plate. It's JLM2—"

"Never mind," Calder mutters. The sound of squealing tires draws our attention and we turn to see a dark-blue sedan speed out of the farthest exit. "She just drove out of the lot."

Glancing his way, I sigh my frustration. "She must've come out another part of the building. Hopefully Elijah can—"

The click of a gun cocking behind us cuts my comment off.

"Face me slowly," a deep voice says.

As we turn, Calder steps sideways, putting himself between the gun and me. A man with buzzed dark hair stands in the exit's open doorway, his silencer-tipped handgun trained on Calder. His cold gaze flicks to Celeste's taillights, then back to us.

Calder pulls me farther behind him. "What do you want with her?"

The guy exhales in a low chuckle. "My employer will be vindicated once he learns the truth. Seeing her—" he nods to indicate me "—while the other *Cass* is speeding away, pretty much seals the deal. Now that I have proof, I can do my job."

"Which is?" Calder asks in an even tone.

Even though my heart is thumping so hard I can hear it, I poke my head around Calder's shoulder in time to see the man subconsciously glance at his gun, then shrug nonchalantly. *Matthews is supposed to take Celeste out?*

I tug lightly on Calder's shirt when he tries to push me behind him once more. "But you didn't actually see her driving that car, did you? We couldn't. So how can you know for certain?"

The man's gaze snaps between Calder and me, irritation evident that I created doubt in his mind. He tightens his grip on his gun, his expression resolute. "I really can't have you two following me or interfering with my plans—"

Matthews suddenly crumples to the ground, his gun dropping to the pavement as he's knocked out. Ben stands behind him, the butt of his handgun still held out. Quickly tucking his gun behind his back, he flashes a satisfied smile. "I never thought I'd have an excuse to cold-cock someone who deserved it. That felt fucking great! You two okay?"

Snorting, Calder shakes his head and retrieves his phone from his pocket. "Elijah, cut the cameras on this side of the building temporarily and erase our presence completely."

"Okay, done. I'll turn them back on once you leave."

After Calder hangs up, he grabs the guy's shirt and Ben helps him haul the unconscious man behind the bushes near the building. Picking up the guy's gun, Calder empties the bullets and pockets them, then looks at Ben. "Text Talia and ask her to call hospital security and leave a tip about a suspicious looking man hanging around the entrance in this parking lot." He kick's the man's booted foot, then puts the guy's empty gun back in his hand just as Sebastian and Den pull up in the cars.

"Where is Celeste? Did she get away?" Sebastian asks through his open window.

I grimace and hope that Elijah checked on the DMV. "Please tell me that Elijah hacked into her GPS too?"

"He did. Call Elijah once you're in the car and he'll give us directions to her location." Sebastian nods to Ben.

"We don't have time to get your car, Ben. Ride with Cass and Calder. Den will ride with me for now."

We follow Celeste's GPS back toward Beacon, except she keeps going, heading for the town of Fishkill.

"She appears to have stopped on the outskirts of Fishkill in what looks like a forest not far from a creek," Elijah says. "Bash is going to take another road and park his car where that road you're on exits. That should stop her from leaving in the opposite direction."

"Got it," Calder says. "Is there a way for you to block Celeste's GPS signal, Elijah? I don't want Matthews following her if the hospital security can't secure him."

"If I block her signal, then we'll be flying blind too if she somehow gets past you or Bash."

"Hopefully we'll get to her before she moves again. Block it now. We can't take a risk that Matthews will follow her here."

CHAPTER NINETEEN

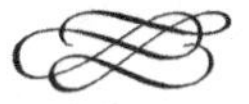

CALDER

I follow the road deep into the woods until I see Celeste's car. Pulling up alongside the empty sedan, I put my car in Park and cut the engine. I retrieve my gun from the glove compartment and load a bullet in the chamber.

"You're not going to shoot her, are you?" Cass asks. "I can't imagine she can get far. She's sick and probably not physically able to outrun you. Between the three of us—"

"You're going to stay here with Ben," I cut her off, my tone clipped." Cass bristles, but before she can argue, I touch her jaw. "She almost *killed* you. I won't give her the opportunity to hurt you again."

Her gaze searches mine, and she must see my unyielding determination, because she folds her arms and sighs. "You have no idea what you'll be walking into.

She's familiar with these woods and you're going in blind. Wait for Sebastian and Den to meet us. Then go with them."

The slightly worn path between mine and Celeste's cars leads somewhere. Checking the safety on my gun, I shake my head. "I can't wait. We don't know if she has another way out of these woods. Tell Sebastian and Den to follow the path I took. They're only a few minutes behind."

Cass grabs my forearm as I open the door. "Take Ben with you."

I eye her death grip on my arm, then shift my gaze to Ben, who's looking at Cass with concern in his gaze. "Stay here with her. Understood?"

Ben's jaw flexes. "The safest place for Cass is with us while I back you up." I start to argue with his stubborn hide, but he shakes his head. "Have you considered that cutting off Celeste's GPS didn't matter? If this Matthews guy is as good as he seems to be, why wouldn't he have downloaded her entire GPS history? That would tell him where she's been before, right? He might already know where we are."

The idea that Matthews could attack Cass and Ben while I'm looking for Celeste is chilling. I don't ever want to take a life, but if it means protecting the ones I love at all costs, there's no contest. I'm not sure if Ben has it in him to do the same. "Contradicting my orders doesn't win you any points, Hemming," I say on a low growl of annoyance.

"You just hate that I might be right." He shrugs and lowers his dark head to check his own gun. "The longer we sit here debating, Celeste is getting farther away."

"Or she could've already set herself up in a position to pick us off like ducks in a carnival game," I grumble, then look at Cass. "Stay directly behind me at all times. Ben will shadow you. No peeking your head around until I tell you it's clear. Got it?"

When she quickly nods, I feel like I've been duped, but I can't see another way to protect her while looking for Celeste. "Close your doors as quietly as possible, then come around and walk behind me."

Stepping onto the path, I hold my gun aloft and scan the trees' thick green foliage while I wait for Cass and Ben to join me.

Once they move into place behind me, I wait for Ben to pull his gun, then step forward, saying quietly, "Watch for roots and rocks. No talking. Tap my shoulder to get my attention."

I hate that we're so out in the open, that Cass is even here at all, and that we don't have back up, but Ben's right...Celeste has a head start and we need to close that gap quickly. It makes no sense why she'd come out here, but she's obviously not in her right mind since she tried to blow up the one person she could turn to for help. Has her illness made her delusional? Even as I trace the recently trampled underbrush and follow Celeste's path, my internal tension grows the deeper into the woods we walk.

Are we being led into a trap? Is this another one of Celeste's twisted mind ploys?

We turn a bend on the path, and I'm just about ready to tell Cass and Ben that we're going back, when I see a clearing up ahead.

I slow my steps and Cass and Ben match my movements. Glancing over my shoulder, I point to the clearing and indicate we're going to approach slowly.

I peer through the woods at the old brick building. We've apparently approached it from the backside, because the only door is small and there's no driveway or road that I can see leading up to it.

A couple of broken seesaws and a merry-go-round indicate a playground. Other than a busted window on the top floor that a bird just flew into, the abandoned building seems strangely protected against the encroaching nature around it. Underbrush has grown all the way up to the sidewalks, but the cement has kept the vines and weeds from completely overtaking the building.

Cass tugs on my shirt, then whispers, "Why in the world did Celeste come to an abandoned school?"

I shake my head. "No clue. Stay here with Ben. I'm going inside to find her."

When I start to walk forward, she doesn't release her grip on my shirt. "Be careful!"

With a silent nod to Ben to keep an eye out, I slowly walk toward the building out of sight from the windows, then peer into the closest one at an angle. I don't see anyone about in the room, just a bunch of school desks. I duck past the bank of windows along the back of the building until I reach the door. Opening it as quietly as I can, I slip inside.

CHAPTER TWENTY

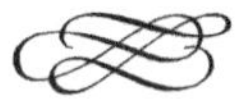

CASS

My whole body tenses the moment Calder disappears inside. After several minutes of silence, I turn and look at Ben. "You should go in there and back him up."

"He said to wait here." Keeping his gaze trained on the door, he snorts, then winces in pain. "He'll do more than break my nose if I let something happen to you."

"He's in there alone." I frown and gesture to the building. "Who knows what Celeste is doing in there."

The muscle in Ben's jaw flexes. "I can't—"

A loud crash inside cuts him off and I jerk my gaze to him. "Go back him up."

Ben's body tenses, but he shakes his head. "He said—"

I grip his arm and hiss, "*I'm* going to kill you if something happens to him. Go help him—"

Calder suddenly yells, "Go around front!"

"Stay out of sight," Ben tells me before bolting toward the front of the building.

I move into the shadow of the trees, my gaze swinging between the front corner of the building that Ben disappeared around and the back door Calder walked into.

Sudden movement out of the right side of the building draws my attention. Just then Celeste jumps down from a window and starts running toward the footpath. She looks tired, her hair pulled back in a messy, thin ponytail.

"Stop." I quickly move into place, intending to block her exit, but Celeste dodges around me with an agility that takes me completely by surprise.

"Ugh!" I take off after her. "Stop running, Celeste."

Celeste doesn't even look back; she tries to run faster. I take a deep breath and dive forward, grabbing her around the waist on my way down.

We both hit the ground hard. I wheeze and try to recapture my breath while dirt and dry leaves float all around. With a strength I didn't expect, Celeste growls, "Get out of my way, Cass. I have to leave!" and shoves me onto my side. Before she can scramble to her feet, I quickly roll back and knock her over.

Crawling to my knees, I straddle her hips and grab her wrists to keep her from smacking me in the face. "Let me go!" she hisses and tries to buck me off, but she's already lost so much energy, she looks so pale and her efforts barely move me at all.

"Get off me. I have to go!"

"You're not going anywhere. You have a lot to answer for," I snap back just as Calder and Ben come running into the entrance of the woods.

Reaching down, Calder lifts me off Celeste, his tone low and strangely calm. "Step back for a minute and let Celeste breathe, Cass."

When Calder sets me down, I realize that Celeste sounded really out of breath. As Ben hauls her to her feet, I see just how emaciated and sickly she looks. She struggles against Ben's hold and an edge of dark ink shows up just below her shirtsleeve.

I step forward and shove her sleeve the rest of the way up, revealing my exact same raven tattoo, even down to the world *Never* along her left forearm. I quickly grab her other arm and look at that wrist. Same tattoo as mine.

Cutting a freaked out look Calder's away, I let my fury fly. "What the hell, Celeste. Is this why you tried to kill me? What did you think would happen? That you could fucking replace me?"

Celeste tries to claw Ben's hold off her arm. "He knows I'm alive now, and he'll be coming for me." She glances Ben's way, her gaze suddenly pitiful and imploring. "Please let me go, Ben. I have to leave. I have to get—"

"Explain yourself." Calder steps around me and

clamps a tight hold on Celeste's shoulder. "Is Cass right?" His gaze narrows to angry slits. "You know you could never fool me, so what fucking purpose did trying to kill Cass serve, other than to feed your psycho-craziness?"

Celeste struggles under both Ben and Calder's hold, then sags in exhaustion. "I'm not crazy. I was sick and needed money. I used an old account that I forgot Phillip knew about. When I realized my mistake, I knew I had to fix it, so I borrowed Cass's credit card info."

"You mean you stole from her," Calder snaps and releases her to fold his arms.

"How did stealing Cass's credit *fix* my father thinking that you might be alive?" Ben demands, shaking Celeste slightly.

"Ow, you're hurting me."

Genuine pain fills her gaze and I say to him, "Release her, Ben. She's not in any condition to go anywhere."

"Answer the question, Celeste." Ben drops his hand, but doesn't step away. "We're waiting."

Pushing the loose strands that had fallen from her ponytail away from her face, Celeste takes a deep breath. "I needed to establish credit elsewhere that tied back to Cass. I knew Phillip would send someone to try to find me, so I had to make sure the path only led him to Cass."

Calder frowns. "Then you could've stopped with Cass's credit. Why try to kill her?"

She shakes her head slowly, her eyes slightly glazed

over. "I knew Phillip would hire the best and that the person would keep digging, so I asked Cass to bring me the money. Having her come to Beacon solidified Cass's connection to an address far from the city, which is why I made sure that anyone snooping through Cass's credit would find that address as well."

"We knew you ordering that water delivery service seemed like a rookie move," Calder mutters, his jaw muscle clenching.

Celeste shifts her gaze to his, her back stiffening. "I never do anything without reason." Her focus quickly slides to me, her eyebrows hiking. "Did you put the money in the lockbox and close it like I asked?"

A sudden realization hits me and rage swiftly rebuilds all over again. "*That's* why you instructed me to put the money in that box and close it. You knew it was fire retardant. Holy shit! You've truly fucking lost it, Celeste."

"I didn't do it for me," she snaps, her sudden teary gaze pinging between the three of us. "What would you do to save your child? How far would you go to keep her safe? My little girl isn't like Phillip or me. She's sweet and innocent and should never have to see the horrible things I've seen or endured at her father's hands. He would use her, abuse her, and never let her go. I knew he would keep hunting us, so I created a credit path to prove you were the one with the separate life in another town, which is what he would report to Phillip. The only thing left was to make sure the only person who knew the truth about me could never be forced to reveal it."

I had to die...to protect a non-existent child? Celeste's delusions are far, far worse than we thought. Which is probably why we were led out here in the middle of godforsaken nowhere. I dart my gaze between Calder and Ben, completely shocked by her diabolical mind. If it hadn't been for Ben, she would've succeeded.

"You don't have a child. There was nothing in your house. No toys. No highchair or baby seat. No sippy cups. Nothing. Did you lose your baby due to your illness? Maybe the stress you're under being on your own or the chemo medicine you're taking has confused you."

"No, you're wrong!" Curling her hands into tight fists, Celeste's eyes widen, an unhinged look of desperation in her gaze as she glances around us. Shifting from one foot to the other, she mutters, "I have to go."

Short of knocking her unconscious to get her back to the car, we need to calm her down. Calder tenses as I take a step closer and say in a much calmer tone than I feel, "Let us take you to the hospital where you can be evaluated, Celeste—"

"Stop calling me that. I'm Cassandra Boswell," she insists as she quickly steps forward and shoves me with all her might.

I stumble back and lose my footing. Calder and Ben each grab a flailing arm and keep me from tumbling to the ground. The moment they pull me forward onto steady legs, Calder grits out, "Son of a bitch, she bolted."

We all take off running down the path after Celeste and back toward the cars. I'm ahead of the guys, but not by much.

"Cass, *wait*," Calder calls after me, but I keep pushing myself beyond the limit. My heart is racing and my lungs burn as if a fire is raging from the inside. I have to protect my own family. Celeste isn't well. I'm the reason she did what she did. Who knows what other paranoid thoughts might enter her head down the road if she gets away. Next time, she might go after someone I'm close to instead of me directly. Everyone could be at risk if she isn't caught and put into a place where she can receive the psychiatric help she needs.

Just as Celeste reaches the end of the path, I panic that she'll get away and say anything to get her to stop. "I believe you, Celeste," I say, panting. "Let us help you."

She stops and just as she turns to face me, a look of relief on her face, she stumbles forward toward me, then crumples to the ground.

Confused as to why she fell, I start to bend and help her, but Calder grabs me by the waist and tosses me behind him like a throw pillow right into Ben's arms. "Get back, Cass," he commands and crouches, quickly pulling his gun.

Something whizzes past my head as Ben pushes me

behind him, ordering, "Get down and stay there. We're flying blind in here."

Calder fires a couple times, but just as he bends down to grab Celeste's hand, a bullet slams into her thigh. She cries out in pain and my heart jumps to my throat as survival instincts kick in. I listen to Ben and drop from my hands and knees to my belly.

From my low position on the leaf-covered path, I can see blood seeping through Celeste's shirt in the chest area, turning the Williamsburg blue color an eerie shade of purple in the dappled sun-light. *God, where's the shooter?* I crane to see him through the trees. Matthews is leaning against his sedan, using its rooftop as a steadying base as he tries to pick us all off.

"Laying down cover. Get her now." The moment Ben straightens slightly from his crouched position and fires his gun in rapid succession, Calder grabs Celeste and drags her back onto the path and out of the shooter's line of sight.

Another barrage of shots zooms through the tree line. Ben jerks sideways, taking a bullet in his upper arm. Leaning up on my knees, I try to grab his pant's pocket and pull him back, but Ben holds his position and says to Calder through gritted teeth, "I think I winged him too. He's using his car for cover."

Calder quickly drops to the ground, peers through the foliage, then props on his elbows before firing off two precise shots. A loud shout of pain sounds just before a heavy thump hits the ground. Calder doesn't hesitate, he fires once more, and then silence mutes all sound.

The moment the gunfire stops and Calder nods to let me know the guy isn't getting back up, I crawl over to Celeste and clasp her hand. Ben drops to his knees and presses his hand to her chest to stop the heavy flow of blood. When he looks at Calder, his jaw flexes and he slowly shakes his head. Unable to help the sob that escapes, my heart squeezes. A life is a life, no matter the person's misdeeds. "I'm sorry, Celeste."

Tears leak down her temples as she tries to catch her breath from the pain, but her hand holding mine is surprisingly strong. "He must never find her."

For Beth's sake, I clasp her sister's hand tighter and nod, telling Celeste what she needs to hear. "Of course."

"Had to get it," she says, squeezing my hand painfully tight. "Promise me, Cass..." She closes her eyes and sucks in a breath, "that you'll keep her safe."

I look at Calder and Ben, my eyes watering, then drop my gaze to Celeste's. "I promise." Just as I nod, she struggles to speak, but her body seizes and she exhales a long deep breath, her gaze losing focus as the light slowly leaves her eyes.

Sebastian and Den come running up. I hear them speaking in low tones to Calder and Ben about Matthews while Calder knots Ben's tie around his arm to put pressure on his wound, but their voices sound muffled and very far away.

I stare at Celeste's still body, my tears hitting our clasped hands. I blink hard to keep from openly sobbing, but when Calder's hand lands on my shoulder, giving it a supportive squeeze, I blubber and reach for Celeste's other hand.

Lifting her clenched hand to cover the one on her chest, I uncurl her fingers to lay her hands flat together, but pause when a piece of paper falls from her grasp.

"Calder?" I whisper to get his attention.

"What is it?" He bends close as I unfold the paper with shaky hands.

There's no name. Just an address written in a cursive script. I shift my gaze to Calder's, eyes wide. "I thought Celeste was saying that *I had to get* what she was asking of me, but..." I look at the paper once more. "I think she was saying, *she had to get this*." I glance back down the path that led to the old school house. "She came here to retrieve this paper. It makes sense now. Celeste had an uncommon way of passing messages with me so no one would know. She probably did it with someone else too." I return my gaze to his. "Poughkeepsie's less than thirty minutes away. We can't leave without knowing for sure, Calder."

He holds my gaze for a couple seconds, then nods. When he pulls me to my feet, I realize the guys have stopped talking. Sebastian looks at the paper in my hand. "Go find out."

He and Den exchange a look, then Den cuts his gaze to Ben. "I hope you understand now the lengths your father will go to. Matthews can never surface."

When Ben slowly nods his agreement, I look down at Celeste and start to speak, but Ben steps forward to touch my shoulder. "We're pretty remote out here, but all the gunfire could've drawn attention. You two need to go now. We'll make sure Celeste has a proper burial on her own land, Cass. Don't worry."

Calder cuts his gaze to Ben's arm. "Make sure you get that looked at."

Ben gives him an "are you kidding me" look. "It was just a graze. I'll be fine. Now go."

Nodding his appreciation, Calder clasps my hand and says to the guys, "We'll be in touch," before we head for his car.

We roll to a stop across the street from a small brick house in a quiet neighborhood.

"You're *not* going to that door alone," Calder says in an unyielding tone.

"Whoever lives there won't be surprised to see Celeste, but they might not trust seeing Celeste with someone else. I mean, who knows what story she fabricated about herself," I say, glancing over my clothes once more to make sure all the leaves and underbrush is completely wiped off.

"We don't even know what this address means, Cass. You know as well as I do that Celeste never would've left her child. Maybe this person has some of Celeste's money and she needed the funds to leave the area for good? They might not want to part with that money now." Rubbing his jaw, he glances toward the house. "The best thing would be for me to ring the bell and pretend I'm looking for someone else. It'll give me a chance to check out who lives there without putting you at risk."

"Or you could freak the person living there out. For all we know, Celeste could be the only one the person living there trusts. It has to be me, Calder."

He clasps my hand when I try to open the door, his hold firm. "We do this together, Cass. Or not at all."

His gaze is turbulent green. It's a defining moment, a turning point where I need to fully commit to the "us" in our relationship. He introduced Raven to the world. It's my turn to take the lead. I squeeze his hand. "Let me talk, okay?"

Nodding his agreement, we get out of the car and walk together to the house.

My hand shakes a little as I lift it to ring the bell.

Calder clasps my free hand and squeezes it briefly before the door opens.

The older woman with a salt-and-pepper pixie cut beams when she opens the door. "Cassandra, you look wonderful, dear." She pauses, giving Calder a wary gaze.

I smile and gesture to him. "He's a big part of why I'm feeling better. This is Calder, my boyfriend, who is also my physical therapist."

The woman's blue eyes spark with intrigued interest as she looks at him. "It's nice to meet you, Calder. If we had PTs as handsome as you when I was a young nurse, I would've gotten in so much trouble." Laughing at her own joke, she pulls the door open and steps back. "Come in."

Just as we step into the foyer, she turns and calls over her shoulder, "Rose, look who's here?"

A child around twelve months old, with a mop of soft curly dark hair awkwardly turns on unsteady legs. Releasing her hold on the stuffed elephant toy attached to a springy coil on a stand-up exercise toy, she smiles and takes a few shaky steps, then falls to the carpet and zooms toward us in a fast crawl.

I quickly step forward and meet her on the carpet, squatting down to smile at her. "Hey, little one," I say as she uses my shoulder to pull herself up to a standing position. I put my hands on Rose's arms to steady her and glance the woman's way. Hating that I don't know her name, I cover my nervousness by asking about Rose. "I can't believe how well she's walking."

"She has learned a lot while you were off getting better the last three months. I know it was hard for you to leave her for so long, but seeing how radiant you look now tells me that it was the right thing to do. I'm amazed at how well those special treatments you were undergoing worked. So...is everything all right now?" She asks, her gaze darting to Calder once more.

I want to ask her how she and Celeste met, how they came to this arrangement, and if it was Celeste's idea that she not know where the woman moved to with the baby. That's a hell of a lot of trust to allow a stranger to care for your child. "Yes, everything is going to be fine." Glancing Calder's way, I smile. "Calder has been my rock, but it was important to me that he learn everything about me, since he's asked me to marry him."

"How exciting! Please tell me you said, *yes*?"

I laugh and nod, offering her a look at my ring while Rose makes happy sounds and leans her belly against my thigh.

"What a unique and beautiful ring," the caregiver *tuts,* giving Calder an approving nod.

Teetering on unsteady feet, Rose puts her arms up and squeals to be picked up. Her sweet face and grabby hands are all the encouragement I need. I quickly pick her up. As I move to stand, I hold her close and inhale her baby smell, then tickle her belly. "You're so adorable. I don't think I'll ever want to stop squeezing you."

Rose giggles, her little fingers folding around mine on her stomach, while her green eyes sparkle with happiness. Pointing to the woman, she chirps, "Ra-Ra." Then she quickly swings back to me and pats my cheeks with toddler sweetness. "Ma-ma."

At that moment, my gaze snags with Calder's. He's watching us intently, his expression hard to read.

"I showed Rose your picture everyday and kept you in her mind while she was learning new words." Gesturing to the sofa, she continues, "Why don't you two have a seat?"

While Calder and I sit down on the couch, she lowers herself into the leather recliner and chuckles. "My younger sister called me Ra-Ra as a toddler. I couldn't get her to call me Roxanne until she was in her twenties." Smiling at Rose, who purposefully turned her back to Calder while she plays with my hair, the woman's eyes fill with pride. "She's been talking up a storm lately. It's been mostly gibberish, but words here and there come out. Of course, "no" is her favorite word."

"What other words have you learned?" I ask Rose as I shift her to my other thigh so she's facing Calder. When she eyes Calder warily and lifts my hair like a curtain, I suppress my laughter. "Rose, I'd like you to meet Calder."

Calder doesn't even bother hiding his amusement. He

chuckles outright as Rose peeks out from behind my hair, only to pull it in front of her eyes once more.

"She's at the wary-of-strangers stage." Roxanne looks at Rose. "Are you playing peek-a-boo, Rosie?"

"Pee-boo, Pee-boo." While Rose giggles at Roxanne and lowers, then quickly lifts my hair back up in front of her face, the older woman leans forward slightly.

"I hope you don't mind that I call her Rosie sometimes. It's my sister's name so it just comes out from time to time."

"Not at all," I say with a genuine smile. "You've taken such wonderful care of her. She's just bloomed."

Roxanne grins, her cheeks blushing with color. "Being your doula always creates a special bond, but my time with Rose these past twelve weeks has made me feel like her grandmother. It has been my pleasure, Cassandra, truly. Oh, where are my manners? Would you two like something to drink?"

"Do you have any tea?"

"Nothing for me, thanks," Calder says.

"Tea it is, dear. I'll be right back." Roxanne gets up a little slowly, then ambles off to her kitchen.

"What are you thinking in that gorgeous head of yours?" Calder asks in a low tone.

The moment he speaks, Rose releases my hair and openly stares at him.

"It's that deep voice, Rose," I loud-whisper against her temple. "Be careful or he'll steal your heart too."

Calder smirks and holds out his hand to Rose. His gaze stays on her as he addresses me. "I thought adoption wasn't on your radar, Raven mine."

When the baby leans forward to pat his knee, I clasp her waist to keep her from falling off my lap, but don't pull her back. I want to encourage her to trust Calder. I watch him grinning as she gives him a shy smile and realize that his questions are his way of gauging my feelings. "I said that I wanted you to have your own children, Calder. I still want that if it's in our future, but little Rose..." I pause as Rose crawls fully into his lap and plops her little butt down. Smiling at him, I finish in a quiet tone, "Rose *is* your blood. We can't let someone else raise your little sister. I think it's best if only our tight circle knows the truth. We'll tell my parents and the other BLACK Security employees that we've been quietly working on adopting for a while."

"This is a huge commitment and adjustment, Cass." He wraps his arm securely around Rose as she settles against his chest. Bouncing his knee slightly, he puts his palm out for her to smack her tiny hand against and holds my gaze. "You were just getting ready to start your business."

"Why can't I do both? You said Raven can do anything. Also, we're in this together, remember?"

The tension in Calder's gaze eases with his smile. "Thank you for putting family first, Cass. The Blakes are so lucky to have you. And yes, you can do anything you set your mind to. I have no doubt whatsoever."

"Here we are." Roxanne walks back into the room and sets a glass of tea on the coffee table for me. "If you want it sweetened, I have sugar cubes."

"Thank you. This is fine."

As I lean over to pick up my glass, Roxanne glances down at my arm. "So should I call you Cass now?"

"Pardon?" I ask, taking a sip of the tea.

She nods toward my arm with the *Never* script and raven tattoo as I set the glass back down. "You were on pain meds at the time, but you were so sincere when you told me about the meaning behind your tattoo. I knew that one day you'd get there."

I exhale a laugh of disbelief at Celeste's audacity. I can't believe she copied everything about me. Thankfully my response sounds more like bemused confusion. "I'm sorry, Roxanne, but I guess I was pretty loopy that day." I lower my arm once more and glance her way. "What did I say?"

Roxanne tilts her head and smiles. "I was so awed by your strength and determination." She points to the word *Never* on my arm. "You said that word inspired you to become *Cass*. And when I asked what you meant, you told me that you never wanted to put yourself before Rose's needs." She moves her finger to the swirled line leading from *Never* and on down to the raven on my wrist. "You said you hoped this would always remind you of your goal to put your daughter first."

She shakes her head and sighs. "I told you then that you had already learned selfless love the moment you had your baby, but you said the Cassandra you were needed to change and you hoped that you would return here as Cass, a strong woman who embodies selfless love. At the time, I thought your anxious self-doubt was the drugs talking, but now that I see you with Rose, you're more relaxed, you're smiling, and you seem genuinely content. I'm so happy to see that you've finally become the *Cass* you wanted to be."

Completely blown away by what Roxanne just revealed, I look at Calder. If he had any concerns, they're gone. He nods as he tucks a yawning Rose more firmly into the crook of his arm. "This little one will absolutely benefit from the amazing woman she is today. I couldn't agree with you more."

Roxanne looks at Rose with affection as the toddler's eyes drift closed. "It appears you've won her over. That's no small feat, Calder. I know it'll be hard, but don't let Raven Rose wrap you too tightly around her little finger."

"*Raven* Rose," I say quietly as I look at Calder and Rose. In Celeste's mind, the raven on her wrist really did represent her daughter. I know that if I look at Roxanne, she'll see the range of emotions scrolling across my face, so I keep my gaze averted.

"At first I didn't understand why you didn't call her by her first name. I mean, with that mop of pretty dark hair, Raven would've been a perfect name, but now that I've gotten to know this sweet cherub, her middle name suits her."

"I agree," Calder says as he glances down at the trusting baby in his arms. "Rosebud is perfect for this little one."

His nickname makes me all teary. I didn't think I could fall even deeper in love with him. *Aww, she is an adorable little Rosebud.*

"Rosebud. I love it." Roxanne smiles as she stands. "Wish I'd thought of it. While she's napping, Cass, why don't you come help me get her things together?"

"Of course." When I follow Roxanne into the hallway, she turns and smiles at Calder and the babysitting on the couch. "I'm going to miss that little tyke so much, but I'm truly pleased she'll be where she belongs." Locking gazes with me, she clasps my shoulders. "I'm also glad that whatever past demons you were running from are now behind you." When I nod my agreement, she squeezes my shoulders, "Oh and before you leave, don't let me forget to give you the three months extra payment you gave me too."

My throat is burning with the need to tell this kind

woman the truth, but I know I can't, so I smile and shake my head. "I won't hear of it. Keep the money. You've been worth every penny. I can't thank you enough for everything, Roxanne."

Calder holds Rose while I buckle her car carrier in the back seat. I've never been more thankful for my godmother duties. Spending quality time with Joey really prepared me for the little things, like understanding how to safely buckle her into a car seat.

"You're quite the pro, aren't you?" Calder muses as I take Rose and arrange the seatbelts around her small, sleeping frame in her car seat.

I look at him as I pull the harness around her chest to make sure it's secure. "When she wakes up in a new environment, it's going to be a hard transition for her. And for us. I'm not deluding myself about that."

He touches my shoulder once I brush the curls away from Rose's forehead to check on her. "We're doing what's best for her. It will all work out."

I nod my agreement. "I know we're doing the right thing. But we'll have to decide together if we're going to tell her the truth when she's older."

Calder touches my chin, and just as I meet his gaze, the street lights pop on behind him, shrouding his face in shadows. "My mom's death devastated me. I don't want her to ever question if she was wanted, Cass. Not for a single second."

The thought that his mother's suicide made him question her love for him breaks my heart. As I kiss his palm, he continues, "We'll tell Rose that we adopted her because we wanted to start our family right away. She'll learn that her birth mother had no other family, and that sadly her mom died not long after Rose was born. Her father was never in the picture. The rest will remain buried with Celeste."

I nod, my gaze misting with appreciation for his empathetic perspective. Calder understands more than anyone how much the truth can tear a child's world apart. Rose needs a stable, loving, and loyal family. We will give her that.

Calder pulls me to my feet, his gaze searching mine. "Do you agree with that truth?"

Nodding, I push up on my toes and press a kiss to his jaw. "You're going to be a wonderful father."

Before I can pull back, he steals a kiss. "Only because of you. And for the love of all that is holy, let's please set a date, angel."

As darkness descends around us, my eyes adjust. Holding his gaze, I raise my eyebrow. "How does Saturday sound? I seem to remember you insisting that would be perfect."

"*Now* she's fine with a short notice wedding." Pulling me close, he exhales a low laugh, then looks over at Rose yawning and rubbing her eyes. "It might take more than a couple days to create Rose's adoption paper trail. We'll want it as clean as possible, so let's work the wedding around that to line the dates up."

This man has such a big heart. I love him so much. Too emotional to say anything, I wrap my arms around his waist and nod.

CHAPTER TWENTY-ONE

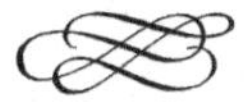

CALDER

Four weeks later

"Are you sure Elijah and Theo have the property covered?" I ask while touching my black bow tie for the fiftieth time. "And where the hell's *my* ear bud?"

Bash gives me a don't-even-ask look, then glances toward the ocean behind us. "Unless someone's coming by boat, we've got you covered."

When I don't react to his sarcasm, he looks at me and frowns. "Why are you so tense?"

I roll my shoulders and wish my custom tux had a little more give. "It took a lot to get us here and I feel—"

"Like it's all going to fall apart?"

"Something like that." I unbutton my suit jacket, then re-button it. "I know it's not rational, but in the back of my mind, there's a scenario where Celeste shows up and all hell breaks loose."

Bash adjusts his cuff under his tux's sleeve, then claps me on the shoulder. "And I thought my wife was the only one with a vivid imagination. Cass is inside being fussed over by Talia, Beth, and Mina. Den hasn't left their side. And Rose appears to be in grandparent heaven. Your family is safe and will continue to be so, Cald. We've got your back."

I look at our families and close friends gathered in the white wooden chairs on the manicured lawn behind Bash and Talia's Hamptons home, and nod to acknowledge Cass's parents when they see me staring. The Rockwells have been a godsend. They cut their trip short the moment we told them we had set a wedding date and were adopting a child, and have been there for us ever since.

Even now, Cass's mom beams with happiness while holding Rose on her lap. I think she adores that Rose's curly dark hair matches hers. She adjusts her granddaughter's little white dress across her knees, then lifts her tiny hand and tells her quietly, "Wave to Daddy."

When Rose turns her head my way, waves enthusiastically, and says, "Da-da," my heart jerks and I cut a proud smile Bash's way.

"Did you hear that?"

He lowers his hand from his ear, clearly listening to one of the BLACK security guys. "Sorry, hear what?"

"I heard it," Ben says from his position behind Bash. "I'm pretty sure she just called you a sheep. Baa Baa."

"Punch my groomsman in his wounded arm," I mutter to Bash, who just ignores me while suppressing his laughter.

Though I think there will always be a bit of rivalry between us, Ben and I have called a truce. Now our interactions are mostly good-natured with an edge of sarcasm.

The last few weeks have been an adjustment for Cass, Rose, and me, but just this week we've gotten the little one through the transition and settled into her new routine. The way Rose has taken to Cass's parents, who've watched her while Cass worked on wedding stuff or had meetings with clients about future shoots, should make the next couple of nights with her grandparents an easy and fun event.

Cass's father kisses her mother on the cheek, then I watch him disappear behind the bank of French doors. I hate that I can't see inside. I'm sure Cass insisted on closing the blinds to keep me in heightened suspense. I'm so ready to hear her say, "I do."

My gaze drops to the two empty chairs up front beside Cass's parents. Decorated with massive black and white ribbons, the chairs are for my parents. Cass insisted we honor their presence. I just wish they could have met her. My father would've adored Cass's all-in nature and my mother would've loved that even though she loves me, she's not afraid to challenge me too. While I wait for the wedding march to start and my bride-to-be to walk through the doors, I say to Bash, "Talia took care of the ribbon on Cass's bouquet, right?"

He nods. "It's from Talia's bouquet, but now died blue per your request. Talia told me to let you know that she gets extra points for not only assuring that it meets your *borrowed* and *blue* requirements, but also because she made sure it matched Cass's black and white wedding theme." When I give him a questioning look, he shrugs. "It's apparently midnight blue."

As I nod and return my attention to the French doors, Bash lets out a low laugh. "You do realize that *you* being as traditional-as-they-come with your requests doesn't negate anything Cass might say or do that is in any way traditional."

"Not worried at all," I say, chuckling at his reminder of our bet, but then all five sets of the French doors open at once, and my cocksure amusement turns serious as the string quartet just inside the doors begins to play the wedding march. I'm a bit surprised by the very traditional song Cass chose, but the fact that it's signaling I'll see her soon is all that matters.

Talia walks out first carrying two bouquets of deep red roses. Beth and Mina follow behind with their rose bouquets. Each lady is wearing her choice of a black sleeveless dress, and with their hair pinned away from their faces, they all look beautiful. I look over at Bash, but his gaze is only for Talia. He's transfixed. It's good to know marriage and becoming parents hasn't dimmed their passion. When Talia meets his gaze and gives him a secret smile, I inwardly chuckle. If anything, it's deepened it.

Once all three ladies come to stand in a line to my right, I nod my appreciation when Talia takes a step back and lays one of the bouquets on the stone patio in front of her to represent Sophie's maid-of-honor position.

As the music slowly dies down, I look up to see my beautiful Cass standing in the doorway with her father, a bouquet of red roses in her hand wrapped in the midnight blue ribbon. Unlike the bridesmaids, her gorgeous hair is flowing in soft curls down her back. I hear the crowd commenting on her simple, unadorned white strapless dress that pinches to a tiny waist before billowing out in a perfect bell shape.

Bash nudges my shoulder, saying under his breath, "She's gorgeous as hell. Can't get more traditional than that, Cald."

Just then, the quartet starts playing a very familiar intro, and a middle-aged woman with silver streaks in her short dark hair steps just outside the doors to belt out the first two words of a song from years gone past. "Aaaaaaat Laaaaaast..."

As she continues to sing in the iconic style of Etta James to chill-inducing perfection, Cass steps forward with her father, her gaze locked with mine and a sweet smile on her face.

The lump in my throat is so knotted, I have to work hard to clear it. She knows my love of old songs, but how did she know this was one of my parents' favorites? This woman has yanked my heart right out of my chest and slammed it back in. The song "At Last" is perfect for our wedding. God, she fucking gets me on so many levels. I've never smiled so big.

Once my bride takes the few steps and starts down the aisle, every person she passes lets out a gasp of delight and a sudden flurry of photos are taken.

The song ends to fascinated gazes locked on my bride. She is gorgeous, no doubt, But it's not until Cass's father releases her hand and I move behind her to pull the train around, that I see why everyone is so enthralled.

The entire back of Cass's wedding dress is solid black, with embroidered silver threads in a distinct pattern that begins just below her tiny waist and goes all the way down the train. The pattern starts as two big arcs at the widest part of her dress's skirt, then narrows into points on either side of her train at the bottom, forming two massive raven wings. It's fucking gorgeous and so beautifully impressive, that I gesture to Bash to help me so he can experience the Cass that I know and love.

The moment he bends down to lift the right side while I lift the left, he looks at me and smiles. Shaking his head, his amazed gaze clearly concedes that my bride is anything but traditional.

Once we've settled the train behind Cass, I take my position beside her as she hands her bouquet to Talia. Nodding to the sandy-haired pastor to let him know I have something to say, I address our family and friends. "Thank you all for sharing this day with us. Cass forgot her 'something old and something new,' so of course I'm going to rescue her non-traditional self."

They all laugh as I pull a gift from my pocket. Holding a delicate chain with three rose gold Victorian style keys in different lengths in front of her, I say, "My father gave this necklace to my mother when they got married and she added the third key to it when I was born. If you look at the smallest key, Cass, you'll see the part that's new."

Cass lifts the keys in her hand and her eyes fill with tears when she sees the rose gold rosebud I had the jeweler form at the top of the smallest key. "It's such a beautiful, sentimental gift. Like your parents are giving their blessing. Thank you, Calder. Can you please clasp it for me?"

While I hook the delicate necklace around her neck, I whisper in her ear, "My parents would've adored you, Cass. The song did me in and the dress finished me off.

I'm so thankful you're finally going to be officially *Raven mine.*"

Once I nod that I'm done, the pastor says a prayer, then speaks about marriage as a blending of families and how our marriage will need to weather the good and the bad. Once he reads another passage, he tells the crowd, "Cass and Calder will now say their own vows as they exchange their rings." Looking at me, he smiles. "Calder, you go first."

I stare into Cass's beautiful brown eyes that are so full of love and think about the life we're making together. Clasping her left hand, for a brief second I forget about our audience and softly kiss her knuckles. When she blushes, I wink at her. "Cassandra Rockwell, you're the most selfless, free-spirited, amazing woman. I will be forever thankful how you stumbled into my life. If it weren't for you, I don't know if I would've ever found my way back to myself again. You make me a better person, because I want you to wake up every day, happy with your choice to be my partner in life."

Cass's eyes soften when I touch her black diamond with my thumb. "I told you that I would always protect you, sweet Cass. And for those times when we're apart," I slide her wedding band of pavé white diamonds outlined with a delicate row of black diamonds up her finger and hook it around the black diamond, "I want you to carry my promise with you everywhere you go."

The moment Cass sees that her wedding band forms the shape of a raven with its neck wrapped around the edge of her diamond, she looks at me with teary eyes and a trembling smile. "It's breathtaking, Calder."

Her hands shake as she takes my hand between hers. "The day you walked into my life was the day I started to believe in me again. The impact you had on me set the path I took and led me to where I am today. You puzzled me out, Calder, and saw right through me, refusing to let me hide the person I was meant to be."

Cass slides a black titanium ring with a thin brushed platinum center band inlaid with a low-key black diamond to match hers. My ring is sleekly modern and classy as hell, but more than anything I fucking love that it means I'm hers and she's mine.

When I fold my fingers around hers and smile, Cass sniffs back her tears. "I never expected I would have an instant family, but nothing about our relationship has been traditional, and I wouldn't change a thing. I love you, Calder Blake. I'm so happy to finally be able to call you my husband."

Hearing Cass say it out loud for the first time is my undoing. I pull her to me and kiss her without a second thought.

"Ahem," the pastor says. "It seems you two skipped right over the "I do" part—"

"We do!" we say in unison, making everyone laugh

and clap so loud that the pastor chuckles and let's them go for a good fifteen seconds before he raises his hands, asking them to settle.

Once our friends and families quiet, his eyes are full of happy amusement as he looks at us. "Calder Jackson Blake and Cassandra Nadia Rockwell, now that you've said your vows, by the power vested in me, I pronounce you husband and wife. You may *now* kiss your bride."

This time I do. With everything I've got, I give the woman I love a kiss worthy of a sailor home for good. When Cass grips my neck and bends us back, saying, "Give me all you've got, Navy," I smile that she's thinking about our first connection in this very house, and plant another one on her to loud whoops, thunderous applause, and a standing ovation.

CHAPTER TWENTY-TWO

CASS

After Calder and I dance one last slow song together while Rose falls asleep on my shoulder, I hand my sleepy child over to my mom's waiting arms. My heart tugs while Mom tucks her little body close against her. I'm going to miss her smell. I can't believe how quickly I became attached as I pat my baby's back and kiss her soft curls.

Now I totally get all the fuss parents make over their kids. Rose might not be my biological child, but she is mine, and I will protect and defend her like any mama bear would. "Sweet dreams, Rosebud. Enjoy spending the weekend with Mimi and Granddad."

I was so thankful that Mom didn't question why we decided to adopt before officially tying the knot. She still doesn't know the details, like the fact that Calder and I took a trip out of town for a day to create an adoption paper trail, or that we just signed Rose's adoption papers as a married couple right after our pastor and Talia witnessed and signed our marriage certificate for the official record. I honestly don't think my parents wanted to question the details behind Rose's adoption, because all it took was one look at Rose's adorable face and they both fell hard for her.

"It was a lovely wedding and reception," Mom says, drawing me back to the present just as Dad leans over and shakes Calder's hand.

"Take good care of our daughter, Calder. She loves you fiercely." His gaze fills with love when he turns his dark head and looks at Mom holding Rose. "And don't you two worry one bit about this little one. She'll be appropriately spoiled rotten."

"Ah, but don't—"

"Shhh, baby girl," Dad interrupts me. "We've got this." Leaning in for a hug, he kisses me on the cheek and whispers, "Your mom's the push over, but wisdom comes with the silver hair at my temples. I'll make sure little Rose stays on her sleeping schedule."

Hugging his neck tight, I nod my appreciation. "Thank you, Dad. I know she'll be in good hands."

Once my parents leave with Rose, Calder looks at me. "Are you ready to start our weekend, Mrs. Blake?"

I smile. "After we say goodbye to Sebastian and Talia."

Calder catches his cousin's eye across the room and inclines his head.

Sebastian nods and walks over to Talia, who excuses herself from speaking with the caterer. As they make their way toward the entryway, I glance up at my husband. "Do you and Sebastian have a BLACK Security nod? Are there other secret-coded looks I should be aware of?"

Calder shakes his head as he escorts me in the same direction. "Apparently, the I'm-ready-to-be-alone-with-my-wife look translates easily."

"Thank you so much for opening your home for our wedding," I say to Talia and Sebastian once they meet us at the front door. While Sebastian claps Calder on the shoulder and they chat about a possible beach trip in mid-September, I hug Talia tight and try not to get misty-eyed. "You know how special your house is to Calder and me, so truly, thank you from the bottom of my heart." Pulling back, I continue, "And thank you for helping me whip this wedding together in a month. I still can't believe we got it all done. Even my custom-made train. I really sweated that it wouldn't get done on time or not turn out the way I'd hoped."

"It's freaking amazing, Cass. I guarantee it'll be the start of a new trend in elaborate trains. Just you wait!" Talia chuckles and pushes my hair back over my shoulder as she glances down at my dress. "I love how the black pencil skirt contrasts with your white strapless top. It's so striking." Amusement fills her expression. "The look on Calder's face when you pulled those hidden ribbons on either side of your waistline, then stepped right out of your massive bell skirt and train was priceless." We laugh together and then she sobers. "And the reason it went so smoothly is because of all *your* check lists. You were so organized with my wedding, I just had to follow your lists and it all came together."

Just then Beth and Mina walk up beside Talia and I hug each of my friends. "Thank you both so much for being here today and pitching in to help with all the crazy last minute details. You made a huge difference and wonderful bridesmaids."

Mina tilts her blonde head and smiles. "I've needed the distraction. It has been my absolute pleasure to help you and Calder, Cass. You're family and Blakes are always here for each other. May you have a wonderful next couple of days together."

Tugging me into a brief hug, Beth says, "I know you've had a lot going on with back-to-back business meetings lately, so will you go on a honeymoon later?"

I quickly nod. "Nailing down my business plan and then meeting with clients to start compiling their ideas so I can come up with some concepts for them is one of the reasons the honeymoon will have to wait until next year.

And now that the wedding isn't taking such a large chunk of my time, I'll be able to focus one-hundred-percent on being a wife, a mom, and building my business."

Beth's eyes soften when I mention being a mom. "Rose is such a sweetheart, Cass. I knew you were playing your wedding stuff close to the chest until you were ready, but it was a shocker when you told me that you and Calder were also adopting a child."

For the first time while talking to Beth, I don't feel guilty about her sister. Yes, I feel sadness for Celeste's death, but not guilt. I know that Rose is exactly where she was meant to be. A part of me will always hope for the day that I'll be able to tell Beth the truth, but as long as Phillip poses a threat, we won't take the risk with little Rose's safety. I'm honoring my promise to Celeste, so that all she did to protect Rose won't have been in vain. "Well, Calder has always maintained that I'm the least traditional person he knows, so it shouldn't surprise you that I bucked the norm on children."

"So true." Beth laughs. "Just so you know, I'm an excellent babysitter. Any time you and Calder need a break, I'm your girl."

I love that Rose has captured Beth's heart too. I smile, my eyebrows hiking. "So you're just going to nix that business dinner to babysit?"

"Absolutely." Beth nods, her smile widening. "Ever since you reminded me that *I'm* the boss, my life has become a lot less stressful. I'm finally enjoying the work, because I don't let it rule my every waking moment."

It warms my heart to see her truly smiling again. I haven't said anything about Celeste's lab report results, but I will the next time Beth seems overly tired. "Ha, be careful what you wish for. I'm so going to take you up on that offer."

Once I've hugged everyone one last time, Calder and I head out. The moment we slide into his car, he hands me a black sleep mask. "Put it on, gorgeous, and no peeking," he says with a stern look.

Intrigued, I slide the mask on. "Is this a precursor to an even more epic night with my Master Puzzler?"

He chuckles and the engine roars to life. "What do those keys around your neck tell you?"

Without my eyesight, Calder's deep, sexy voice rolls over me like the beginning melody of a soulful song. I feel myself smiling as I touch the keys. "That you will always have my heart."

Calder captures my hand and kisses my knuckles. "You always seem to read my mind. You might want to settle into the seat and take a nap."

I turn toward his voice. "We're not going that far, are we? What if Rose freaks out? I don't want to be too far away. She's had so much transition...I really hope she can handle waking up at my parents' house."

"Rose will be fine, Cass. She's been to your parents'

place plenty of times. Kids are resilient as long as they know they're loved." Calder squeezes my fingers. "And no, we're not going to be hours away, I promise."

Exhaling to relieve the motherly tension in my chest, I nod. "Okay, then."

"Give in to all that champagne and close your eyes, wife. We'll be there before you know it."

"Yes, husband," I say, blowing him a kiss.

He chuckles, his voice dropping to a husky purr. "I can't wait to test the limits of this sudden obedience."

THE ELEVATOR PINGS and Calder clasps my hand, leading me off. "Step right here and stay for a second."

I'm surprised the entryway outside our room isn't carpeted—I can feel the hard floor underneath my heels. I smirk, thinking how quiet the hotel was when we entered downstairs. It's probably because everyone stopped to stare at the sexy guy in a tux leading the woman in a mask upstairs. *Haha, the scenarios running through their heads must be hilarious.*

I let out a surprised squeal when Calder quickly lifts me in his arms and cradles me against his chest as he walks forward. "You can take off your mask now, Raven mine."

When I whip off my mask, expecting an extravagant

hotel room, I'm surprised at the skyline view of New York city sprawled out before me like artfully crafted Christmas tree lights.

"What a beautiful view, Calder," I gasp, staring at the city beyond the outdoor patio with gorgeous ferns and other plants around cushioned furniture.

"I hope you love it," he says, then turns fully around. "Welcome home, Mrs. Blake."

Shocked, I tear up at the beautifully decorated penthouse. The style is a bit more modern than the estate home, but with soft touches of textured pillows and pops of color it feels homey and inviting. The overall look is perfect for a home in the heart of the city. "This is ours?" I ask slowly.

Calder kisses my temple. "We'll switch out whatever you don't like, but you said you wanted to be in the city. This place has three bedrooms, so plenty of room for our family and guests. And we're just a few buildings down from Bash and Talia's place."

I quickly glance up at him. "You're not selling your family's estate house, are you?"

"Hell no." He shakes his head. "That's our home, Cass, but it makes sense for us to have a place closer to work for both of us. I'll also be able to get to Gil's easily from here, so I sold the other apartment near his gym."

Setting me down, he rests his hands on my shoulders.

"I want you to always come home to me, no matter how long a day you've had."

I blink back my emotions. This man's thoughtfulness is breaking me today. Truly. Pushing up on my toes, I kiss his jaw. "I love you, Calder. Thank you for being so wonderful and thinking about our family."

Before I can lower myself back to the wood floor, he captures my jaw and presses his lips to mine. The possessive thrust of his tongue enticing me to play sets my body on fire. Just when I place my hands on his lapels to yank him closer, he breaks our kiss and shakes his head, murmuring, "Whenever you get that close, I can't help myself." Kissing my forehead, he clasps my hand and pulls me back toward the elevator. "Come with me."

Intrigued, I follow him into the elevator. Calder pulls me in front of him and wraps his arms around my waist, then pushes the button for a floor below ours. As the elevator doors close, I glance over my shoulder in confusion. "Where are we going?"

He kisses the tip of my nose. "Pay attention, Raven mine."

I face forward and just as the elevator doors open, soft lighting pops on, filling the empty loft style apartment.

Calder pushes me forward until I'm standing on the polished wooden floors. "Just like on our penthouse floor above, the sunlight in this place is amazing. I didn't think we'd get the walls knocked out in time, but we did. Welcome to your new studio, Raven."

I jerk my gaze up to his, my lips trembling. "Are you serious?"

He smiles down at me, folding his arms tighter around my waist. "The title is in your name. This is my wedding gift to you."

"I'm just...this is too much, Calder."

He shakes his head. "No, it's entirely selfish. I want you to be able to do what you love. If you're happy, then I'm happy. It's as simple as that." Releasing his hold, he sets a keycard in my hand, then pushes me forward. "Go on, check out your new space."

As I step forward slowly, still a bit in shock, I glance back at him. "You're not worried about security?"

He folds his arms, his expression turning serious. "Every client you work with will be quietly vetted, Cass. That is my requirement. Even though they would need a special card and code to get up to the top floor, your clients would only know we live upstairs if you tell them. For obvious reasons, we won't be sharing our address with anyone but close family members."

Nodding my agreement with his plan, I walk through the massive space, photo shoot concepts popping into my head so fast, my heart races. I move toward the bank of windows that span the entire wall and see that this apartment also has its own deck as well. "You can see forever across the city," I say, grinning like crazy. "I imagine the light will be so amazing in this space."

"Check out the view now," he says, hitting a button on his phone to turn the lights off.

I gasp at the panoramic view the wide space allows. "It just steals your breath."

"She certainly does," he says right behind me as he sweeps my hair away from my neck and presses his lips to my warm skin.

I smile when his hands slide my skirt up my thighs and lean against him, threading my fingers in his hair. "Have you ever had sex above the city?"

His hands halt and he rumbles in a low tone, "Have you?"

Laughing at his possessive question, I sigh. "Not with you."

Before I can say another word, he spins me around and sets me against the glass. "You have no idea how much I love the fact that you're officially off the market. You're fucking dangerous for my health, Cass."

I touch his jaw and pull him close, loving that he instantly molds his hard body against mine like we're two perfectly fit puzzle pieces. "You always make me pant, Calder. Your heat, your smell, your dominance." I trace my finger down his chin, tugging his bowtie apart, then the top button of his shirt. I smile when his Adam's apple moves with his swallow and kiss his neck, then whisper against his mouth, "Everything about you turns me on. And now that I have your name, what are you going to do differently to me as Mrs. Calder Blake? Hmmm?"

He cups my ass and presses his erection against me. "Never fucking let you go, angel. Good thing you love me, because you're mine now."

"I was serious about having sex above the city," I say and pull open his belt, then his pants button.

Gripping my wrist before I can go any further, he exhales a harsh breath, clearly trying to remain calm. "There's nothing I want more than to fuck your beautiful body into complete exhaustion, Cass. But I want our first time as a married couple to be in our new home, not in an empty room that echoes."

"You really are traditional, aren't you?" I say, with a surprised laugh.

He snorts. "I'd rather not be reminded of that night Bash put the baby monitor up to our bedroom door. I could do without hearing us having sex *in stereo*."

My sudden laughter bounces off the bare walls like crazy, but it's the "see what I mean" look on Calder's face as he spreads his hands wide that makes me laugh harder. Finally calming down, I sigh my disappointment. "Fine, but the moment I get this place decorated, your ass is—"

He captures my lips in a possessive kiss that lingers too long for a man who has no intention of having sex. I step forward, not wanting to stop kissing his mouth as he pulls away. "I'll be all yours, ready and willing to do whatever dirty deed you want, Mrs. Blake."

Damn it, but I know he's right. "Promise?"

The carnal look he gives me sets my insides on fire. It'll be a miracle if my delicate panties don't melt away from the heat. In order to distract myself, I try to focus on the space once more. "Thank you for this wonderful gift, Calder. I can see us using this space for more than just my work. We'll use the one bedroom to move my equipment out of the way when it's not being used."

Moving away, I gesture to the far corner. "We'll set up a seating area with soft cushy couches and chairs over there, and add an island and barstools in the open kitchen. Then we can use it for office parties, Blake family get togethers, ladies nights out, and birthday parties with swinging space for a piñata. I'll be the hostess with the mostest!"

Redoing his pants, he moves to stand beside me and smiles. "I'm glad to see you're already off and running with ideas. We still need to have a speaker system installed in this space. Speaking of which...let's go upstairs. I have something else to show you."

He clasps my hand and pulls me into the elevator. As we move up to the top floor, I ask, "Aren't we going to get our luggage out of the car?"

The door slides open and Calder gestures to our

overnight suitcases waiting for us just inside the door. "And like that, I made them magically appear."

Laughing at him, I head straight for my suitcase, calling over my shoulder, "Your wedding present is in my case. Just so you know...it's not anything extravagant like a new home." While I turn my suitcase on its side and unzip it, I'm so nervous that his gift will seem lame that I ramble, "Whatever you're going to show me, I hope it's something small. I'm not sure if I can handle another big present, Calder. I think you've got my birthday and Christmas covered for the next...oh, thirty years or so."

Music starts to flow through the apartment sound system with crystal clarity just as I pull out Calder's present. I smile at the Otis Redding song "Sitting on the Dock of the Bay" currently playing and turn to face my husband.

He's standing by the turntable record player, his hands held toward it, excitement in his gaze. "It's awesome, right? One great thing about getting this place ready for us, I made sure the sound system guys set up the turntable to play through the house speakers. Now that I hear how good it sounds, I'm definitely going to have this done at our other house."

I smile, feeling a bit better about my gift for him. He's so excited, he doesn't notice what I'm holding until I'm standing right in front of him. "What do you have there, sexy?" he asks, a smile tugging on his lips.

I hand him the gift. "Open it."

Once he carefully tears away the wrapping paper, I point to the album sleeve. "Do you see her signature?"

"This is amazing, Cass. Where did you get it? My father's signed album didn't survive the years of use and tragically got thrown out. I've tried, but failed to find another signed version to replace his. Getting anything less wasn't acceptable."

"So you missed out on years of listening to this amazing voice in vinyl?" I *tsk* and shake my head. "I got this one in an auction. It was one heck of a bidding war, since there were supposedly less than a dozen of these signed, but I prevailed. I felt so lucky when I saw it up for bid. I had to get it for you, since I didn't remember seeing it in your collection."

With a huge smile, Calder puts away the Otis Redding album, then sets the new record on the turntable. Carefully laying the needle on the vinyl, he takes my hand as Etta's amazing voice pumps through the speakers, singing our wedding song.

"At Last," he says quietly, pulling me close.

As we slowly spin to the song that will always remind me of our wedding day, my husband kisses me with such soft, sweet kisses, my heart is full and I feel incredibly blessed. When a tear trickles down my cheek, Calder pauses and tilts my chin. "Are you okay?"

I nod and smile. "I'm just so happy. Today has been... magical. I never want it to end."

He nods toward the window and releases me. "Go open the doors and we'll enjoy the deck for a bit before the rain comes. I'm going to put some more music on."

The doors leading out to the deck are actually massive windows that slide sideways, opening half the "wall" up to the deck. The moment, I open them, sounds of the city below flow into the apartment. "Wow, these windows are super sound proofed."

I grin back at Calder the moment I step out onto the deck and can still hear the music. "You put speakers out here too? God, I love this!" Closing my eyes, I lift my arms wide under the summer night sky and soak in the smells and sounds as the breeze of the coming storm brushes along my skin.

Calder captures me mid-spin, his warm hands circling my waist as he pulls me close. The moment we connect, I open my eyes and smile that he has shed his jacket, tie and shirt before he turned off the inside lights, leaving us in twilight darkness. When the song he's queued up begins to thump in a slow, erotic beat through the speakers all around us, my heart rate quickly rises in anticipation.

While the provocative sensuality of "I Wanna Kiss You All Over" by Exile washes over me, I nod my appreciation of the era he chose. Thunder rumbles way off in the distance, but all I feel is the electricity sparking between us as Calder lightly traces his fingers down my arms. Capturing my hands, he lifts them and locks my fingers behind his neck, then settles his hands on my hips. His gaze never leaves mine as he pulls me flush to his body. Aligning my body with his, he begins to move our hips in a slow, sexual roll as we turn to the music.

The tiny hairs on my arms stand up as the evocative words combine with the warm summer air teasing my skin like a lover's breath. The carnal look in his gaze leaves me breathless right before he lowers his lips to my jaw line. Kissing and nipping at my skin, my handsome husband spins me around at a bone-melting, jaw-grinding pace.

I hold back my sighs of pleasure, not wanting to miss any of the arousing words of the song as his fingers flex on my hips, directing me to his every whim. I let my head fall back when his hot mouth slides to the hollow of my throat. All the while Calder's hips fuse even closer with mine, mimicking exactly what he wants to do to me. My insides melt and I twine my fingers in his hair, clasping him closer. This leisurely, sensual seduction is wrecking havoc on my nervous system, yet I love it so very much.

True to the song he chose, his lips explore every part of me.

As he kisses my shoulder, I exhale a gasp of excitement when the zipper on my dress slowly slides open. We never stop moving to the sexual beat and with each undulation of my hips, my dress moves on its own down my body.

The moment the cloth hits my feet, Calder doesn't miss a beat. He keeps us skin-to-skin as he lifts me out of the dress and turns just as the song "Heaven" by Bryan Adams begins to play.

I don't care that I'm half naked out in public. I'm being masterfully seduced by the man I love. This...truly is heaven.

The moment he pops the hooks on my strapless bra and it falls to the floor and the heat of his chest fuses with mine, the tiny hairs on my arms stand up. I moan as my sensitive nipples brush against the bit of hair on his hard, muscular chest. The song's seductive words completely pull me in and I whisper in a husky voice, "I can't stand it. Kiss me, Calder."

He cups my jaw and just when his mouth covers mine and his tongue slides deep in aggressive dominance, warm raindrops hit our faces.

Calder starts to pull back, but I push up on my bare toes. My fingers dig into his scalp and I pull him closer to deepen our kiss.

Rumbling his approval, he palms my ass with one hand and the other cups the back of my head as he plunders my mouth with a primal kiss that feels both territorial and deeply emotional.

With each drop of water that hits us, our hands move

faster, along with our breathing. "Fuck! I wanted this to last longer," Calder rumbles against my mouth, even as he pops the side strings on my flimsy underwear with quick flicks of his wrists.

"I'm so ready, the rain hitting us will feel dry in comparison," I ramble as I undo his pant button and yank down the zipper.

Calder chuckles and wraps his arms tight around me. "God, I love you."

Thunder rumbles much closer now. I cup his jaw and stare into his handsome face as drops of rain run down his forehead and along his nose. "I'm not going inside. Want to roll the dice with me?"

A sexy grin tilts his lips before he sheds his clothes, then tugs me down onto the round lounger. Pulling me close, he hooks a leg over mine. "You wanted to make love above the city." He presses a lingering kiss just under the curve of my jaw and I tilt my chin up so I can feel the full heat of his mouth. It's such an arousing contrast to the fat, cooling raindrops hitting our skin. "Never say I don't deliver in spades, Raven mine."

Folding my arms around his neck, I kiss his mouth, then whisper against it, "You always deliver. On so many levels."

The haunting song "Hallelujah" by Jeff Buckley starts playing just as Calder tugs my damp hair back to allow him fuller access to my neck. I smile that the sexual undertones in the song mirror our current activity and wrap my legs around his hard body to encourage a deeper connection.

Calder lowers his head to my breast and sucks hard on my nipple, then does the same to the other one before lifting my thigh higher up his back as he slides inside me.

Mewling my pleasure, I dig my nails harder into his shoulders as he presses me deep into the cushions. With the music teasing our ears, the storm heightening our passion, and the rain fusing our bodies together, I enjoy the intimacy of his purposefully slow possession. The unhurried movement of his hips against mine feels deeply soulful, communicating textured layers of emotive feelings.

I gasp, my toes tingling and muscles tightening as my ecstasy builds.

Lightning flashes, and even though it's in the distance, I feel the electricity scatter along my skin. My pulse jumps with the impending danger. My breathing ramps and deep in my chest my heart races as my orgasm unfurls through my body. I shake as the tempest rolls through me, sending electrical currents to all my erogenous zones. When I cry out, my elation elevates at the sound of Calder's masculine groan. "Holy fuck, Cass!" as he climaxes right along with me.

We both lay there spent, our beating hearts making my whole body vibrate in time to their rapid pace. As the rain dies down and the storm moves away, in the pocket of silence the provocative song coming to an end leaves behind, I realize that Calder and I just reached a level of intimate completeness we never have before in our lovemaking.

Maybe it's because we're newly married. Maybe it's because of the storm and the danger its arrival evoked. All I know is, I'm so speechless that I kiss my husband's neck as I try to gather my thoughts.

Calder must've felt the same because he rolls us onto our sides, then tucks my back against his chest, his left arm wrapping around my waist to lock me against him.

The steamy night air dries our skin quickly as he traces his fingers along the curve of my shoulder, then down my arm to lace his fingers with mine.

Smiling, I fold our hands toward my mouth and kiss his wedding ring. "Just so you know...we are so having sex outside more often."

Calder's chuckle vibrates against my back. "Bash mentioned renting a big place on the beach in Martha's Vineyard in September. Maybe we could sneak off before sunrise for some lovin' on the beach."

"Hmmm, sounds gritty," I say, snickering.

"You have no idea, *wife*." Chuckling, he draws me even closer, his voice dropping to a purr in my ear. "I really fucking love saying that."

Nodding my agreement, I lift his hand and run my

finger over his ring. "When I couldn't find a ring that fit what I wanted, I had this one specially made for you. Did you figure out why yet?"

Calder spreads his fingers to stare at his ring. "It's classy but very masculine. I love it, Cass." Turning his hand over, he looks at the back. "Going to tell me what I'm looking for?"

"Take it off," I say, grinning.

Calder does as I suggest and squints as he stares inside the ring. "Is there an inscription that I'll need a black light to read?"

I laugh. "No, but that would've been amazingly cool if I had done that."

"It's probably too dark out here for me to see it." He turns the ring around, staring at all sides.

When he starts to put it back on, I take his ring and roll over, facing him. "Oh no. You're going to figure this out, Mr. Master Puzzler."

Calder's brows pull together with my challenge and he takes the ring and really inspects it. When he pushes on the edge with his thumbnail, his eyes light up that the platinum band moves apart from the main ring. Using both thumbs, he gently nudges the center ring down from its snug fit in the center of his titanium ring until he separates the two.

Lifting the platinum ring up, he reads the black inscription on its side. "Always my Master Puzzler."

"Turn it around," I say, gesturing for him to flip the ring.

When he does, I point to today's date inscribed in fancy script. "Not only is it sentimental, but...ahem, you'll never forget our wedding anniversary."

"No worries there, angel. This date is etched in my memory. I love my wedding ring's uniqueness, but *you're* what makes it truly special." Calder slides his ring back on and leans on his elbow to kiss my nose. "Thank you for agreeing to share the rest of your life with me. And for being Rose's mom. You're the best mother, which doesn't surprise me one bit." He tucks a damp strand of my hair behind my ear, his thumb tracing my jawline. "You are the love of my life, Cass. I wouldn't want to travel this marriage, kids, and whatever-comes-next road in life with anyone else by my side."

My chest tightens with emotion as I cup his hand and press it against my jaw. "Mrs. Calder Blake and mom to little Rose are the best titles in the world. I love everything they represent: love, loyalty, family, but more than anything, this is what I love most about you both." I curl my finger to entice him closer. The moment he leans in, I pounce on him, throwing him back onto the cushion. "You're *all* mine!"

"Who knew you were such a possessive minx," he says as he quickly rolls me under him.

I fold my arms around his neck and look up at my

wedding ring before I pull him close. "You might be the Master Puzzler, but I'm the cunning Raven. I will always keep you on your toes."

He quickly nips at my shoulder, a pleased purr escaping his mouth as he kisses the pain away. "I'm sure you will, but that doesn't change the fact you will also always be *Raven mine.*"

CHAPTER TWENTY-THREE

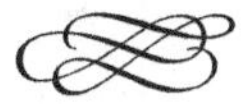

CALDER

Trying to get Rose to stay in a stroller by the front door while her mother is fussing with new picture frames she's arranging on the mantel in our penthouse seems pointless.

"As long as Rose sees you buzzing around that mantel, she's not going to stay in her stroller without a fuss."

"Don't give her a choice." Cass doesn't even look my way as she tilts the antique style frames this way and that, then moves the tallest frame from the end of the mantle to the middle. "She will only pitch a fit about it if you react. She knows she has you wrapped around her little finger."

I stare down at Rose, who's grabbing at the strap belting her into the stroller with a look of angry frustration on her tiny face. "Stay, Rosebud."

"She's not a dog," Cass says, laughing.

I quickly glance at my phone for the time. "Let's go, Raven mine. I want to make it to the airport in plenty of time. We don't know what traffic will be like."

"Talia and Sebastian won't leave without us, Calder. That's the great thing about owning your own plane."

Rose keeps straining to see her mom, so I push the stroller over toward Cass. The tyke instantly stops fussing, a smile lighting her sweet face the moment she can see her mom. "See, problem solved."

Cass glances over her shoulder and smirks at Rose clapping her hands. "Yep, she's got you right where she wants you."

Grunting, I look up to see what she's doing and my gaze instantly focuses on the tall picture frame. It's a photo of my parents dancing on the beach. My mom is mid-spin, the loose sand kicking around her bare feet as she laughs up at my father. I'm instantly transported back to that day, and the sound of my mom's laughter and dad gently chiding her to pay attention to his instruction makes me smile. The photo's in a softer focus than I remember, but the softness gives it a throwback, nostalgic feel that makes you want to know their story.

When I move closer to inspect the photo—that I'd torn to bits as a child after my mother died—I realize that whatever Cass used to hold the pieces together not only made the tear lines disappear, but gave the photo its old-time look.

I quickly scan the other pictures. There's one of me as a kid fishing with my father, one of Cass with her sister as teens, another of Cass's parents giving Rose a sweet kiss on either cheek. The next one is of Cass and me on our wedding day. One of Cass and Talia at college graduation, and one of Cass, Rose, and me at a BBQ that Bash and Talia hosted at their Hamptons home a couple weeks ago. All have the same artistic flair coating the photos, making the obvious love of family in them timeless.

"You asked me how I knew about your parents' favorite song." Cass's ponytail swings as she points to the photo of my parents on the beach. "It was written on the back of this photo."

"Sneaky," I say as I wrap my arm around her waist. "They were so happy that day. It was truly one of my best memories. Thank you for rescuing it."

Rose starts to fuss, so Cass unstraps her and lifts her up on her hip. Taking the photo of my parents down, she shows it to Rose. "These are your other grandparents, little Rose." She looks at me. "What would they have wanted to be called as grandparents, do you know?"

I start to shrug, then remember what I'd called my father's parents. "Papa Jack and Mama Becca most likely. Yep, that's what they would've gone by."

Nodding, Cass holds the photo closer to Rose. "Meet Papa Jack and Mama Becca. They loved your father so much and are sad that they didn't get to meet you, Rose."

Rose smiles and flattens her hand on the glass, smudging it with her fingerprints. "Pop-pop."

Cass and I laugh and I lift Rose into my arms, smiling at her expressive face. "Close enough, Rosebud."

Cass puts the photo back on the mantel without wiping the glass. "I wanted them to be the first to know."

Bouncing Rose on my hip, I glance her way. "Know what?"

"About their grandbaby."

Smiling, I tickle Rose's belly, loving the sound of her squeals of laughter. "I think the smudges Rosebud left behind clued them in."

Cass brushes Rose's dark curls back from her face to kiss her forehead. "Yep, little Rose leaves a bit of herself behind wherever she goes, but I was actually referring to their newest grandchild."

My heart jerks and I snap my gaze to hers, my arm pulling Rose closer. "Are you serious?"

"Surprise!" She spreads her hands and nods, her smile wide. "Apparently not worrying about getting pregnant was the magic formula."

I step close and fold my arm around her, kissing her temple. "I told you it would all work out."

She snorts and looks up at me. "Because you have the answer to everything?"

"I do." I flash a cocky smile. "It's called the magic touch."

"Gah, only you would interpret my comment that way." Pursing her lips in amusement, she wraps her arm around my waist. "In seven and a half months, we're going to have two little Blakes to shower our love on. My parents are going to be ecstatic!"

"I can't wait to tell the gang when we get to the beach," I say, unable to stop grinning.

Cass quickly shakes her head, her brow furrowing. "Not yet, Calder. I won't feel comfortable telling others until we're past the twelve-week mark. With my tilted uterus, my pregnancy is more precarious."

"Not even Talia?"

She squeezes my waist. "This is our family secret for now."

Nodding my understanding, I hold her gaze. "Make sure your doctor appointments are on my calendar."

"It's not necessary for you to—"

"I will be at every single one, Cass."

Emotion flickers through her brown eyes. Just as she starts to speak, Rose pats both our faces, chirping, "Mama, Dada."

"Awww, sweet baby." My wife takes the baby and tucks her little face against her neck, then looks at me, worry creeping into her expression. "I hope everything will be all right."

"It will be." I run my fingers down her ponytail, then rest my hand on the back of her neck. "But no matter what happens, I'll be there every step of the way."

She looks up at me, relief filling her gaze. "Thank you for being strong for both of us."

"Gather round, girls." Wrapping my arms around them, I kiss Cass's hair and whisper against her ear, "I love you, angel. So fucking much."

CHAPTER TWENTY-FOUR

CALDER

Ben sets a cooler of beer down, then plants his beach chair next to mine in the sand. Handing me a beer, he sits and twists the cap off his own. "So how's fatherhood?"

I instantly jerk my gaze his way, thinking Cass might've told him about her pregnancy, since he is kind of the family doctor. But Ben's looking at Rose as she squeals with happiness while her mom and Beth swing her feet in the bubbling surf.

I nod toward the massive sandcastle he and I just built together with Rose and twist off my own beer top. "Nice design. Did they teach sand art in med school?"

When Ben snorts, then shifts his gaze to me and I see his question's sincere, I look at my family and smile. "It'll change the whole way you look at your life, that's for sure."

"I want to be a part of her life, Calder." Ben brushes sand off his knee, then rests his wrist on it as he squints against the hot sun. "She's my sister too."

"That's good." I watch Beth capture Rose in her arms, then begin to spin, moving faster with Rose's excited giggles.

"What's that supposed to mean?" Ben frowns, his gaze straying to Beth. "Are you ever going to tell Beth the truth?"

Beth has watched Rose for us a couple of times, and I'd bet a hundred bucks she has already asked Cass when we'll need her help again. Once she finally slows to a stop and starts to hand Rose to Cass, I watch my wife turn our daughter and set her upright on Beth's hip. The moment Cass begins talking in earnest to Celeste's sister, I look at Ben.

"You will be involved in our daughter's life. Her birthdays. Important milestones, etc. The uncle who listens to her complain about her parents. That's what godparents usually do."

Ben chokes on his swig of beer. "Godparent?"

I smile as Beth does a little hop, then throws her free arm around Cass's shoulders, giving her a hug. Lifting my chin in their direction, I say, "That's what I call a happy reaction. Beth is ecstatic. If you're not up for that kind of commitment—"

"No, I'm honored."

When I lift a doubtful eyebrow, Ben gestures toward his castle masterpiece. "Did I not just build an entire sand hotel for a toddler?"

I tilt my beer toward him. "Fair point."

"So *are* you going to tell Beth?" Ben asks, his gaze following Cass, Rose, and Beth as they head off for a walk down the beach.

I stare at Beth chatting with Cass. "As her godmother, Beth will get to be as close as she wants to be with Rose, but to protect my daughter, no, Beth can never know the truth." Sliding my attention back to Ben, I narrow my gaze. "And if Phillip dares to send someone else to follow my family again, even prison won't be safe for him."

Ben rubs his arm where he'd been shot, his gaze shifting to the ocean as he takes a swig of his beer. "As far as I'm concerned, he'll get what he deserves."

Once his beer is gone, he gives me the side eye. "I just realized why Beth and I were invited to come for the day. When do I get to come for the whole week like Sebastian and Talia?"

I snort and shake my head, swallowing some of my beer. "Don't push your luck, bro."

His gaze locks with mine for a second, then he chuckles. "But that's what I do best. I thought you would've figured that out by now. Speaking of which...when are you going to give me that blood sample?"

"What is your deal?" I snap, frowning at him. "Bash told me you didn't ask anyone else for a sample."

Ben rubs his neck and sighs. "Look, our father has Rheumatoid Arthritis. It has gotten worse the last couple of years. You're in the field from time to time, and a strong grip is important in many aspects of security, including handling a gun."

When I give him a mind-your-own-fucking business look, he shakes his head. "This isn't about me trying to bench you, Calder. I just want you to know if you inherited his RA genetic markers."

I turn my gaze to my family and take a long swig of my beer. "I don't want to know, Ben. If it happens, it happens."

"The thing about RA is, if you ignore the pain and let it progress, it can't be reversed. There are good medicines on the market today that can arrest RA symptoms, but knowing what to look for and early detection is key. Just consider it. I'll do all the legwork in getting it to the lab."

Wouldn't that be the fucking cherry on top if Phillip passed his crappy genetics on to me? I want to punch Ben for putting the thought in my head, but as I watch Cass walking up the beach with a tuckered out Rose sleeping on her shoulder, being the best that I can be for my family is most important to me. I glance his way and finish off my beer. "I'll think about it."

Nodding, Ben hands me another beer and shakes his head, his mouth quirking in amusement. "I can't believe I'm going to be my sister's godparent."

I shrug. "I'm her father."

Ben laughs and holds his bottle up in salute. "Here's to one hell of a family tree."

Snorting, I clink my bottle against his. "It might be all knotty and snarled, but I wouldn't have it any other way."

Cass

AFTER WE FINALLY GET THE girls to lie down under the baby tent for a short nap, Talia and I collapse in the seats Calder and Ben vacated. "While Ben and Beth are off hunting shells to impress the girls with once they wake up, I'm getting a drink." Popping open the cooler, she cuts her gaze my way and huffs. "I can't believe they drank all the beer. That's the only reason my redheaded butt is still out here."

I snicker as I finish winding my ponytail into a bun. "And look, you somehow managed not to burn up in a crispy poof. I really wish Mina could've come with Josi. All three little girls would've had the best time together."

"I wish I knew what was going on with Mina. She's never around when I try to call lately. Of course we invited her to come, but she texted that Josi had a cold and she'd plan to come next time we had a family get together." Talia sighs as she digs through the cooler. "All I see here is water. Want one?"

"Yes, please. Beer just makes me thirsty in the heat."

Handing me a water bottle, Talia pulls one out for herself as our husbands walk up, apparently bored with throwing a football back and forth.

"I won," Calder says.

"Nope, I clearly won. Cass said the word *traditional* during her vows."

"What are you two going on about?" Talia asks.

After Sebastian explains the bet he and Calder made, Talia rolls her eyes and proclaims, "It's a draw."

When both guys start to argue, she narrows her gaze. "First of all, did you plan on being my officemate, Calder?"

"We made the bet before that door between your offices was installed," Calder admitted.

"That *door* makes your bet null and void." Turning to her husband, she says, "By the way, there's no beer for you. You can thank the *lush brothers* for drinking it all."

"I can't believe you guys were betting on me," I mutter as I check my phone for the time. Calder's last text pops up, reminding me of the hilarious photo he texted me of Rose tasting a lemon for the first time.

When I show it to Talia, she laughs. "Aren't kids so funny?" Glancing up at Calder, she smirks. "*Master Puzzler*, huh?"

Her gaze shifts to her husband, an auburn eyebrow cocked. "Tell me he didn't rag on you about 'Rainbow Master.'"

"Rainbow Master and Master Puzzler." Calder brushes sand off his six-pack abs, then gives Talia an arrogant grin. "Hmmm, I'm sensing a dominant theme here, right, Bash?"

When Sebastian smirks and folds his muscular arms against a tan chest, I roll my eyes. "Rainbows and puzzles? The only theme I'm seeing is that our men never grew up."

Just as Talia bursts out laughing, Joey rolls over and starts to cry. Her father quickly swoops her up, drops a kiss on her cute little red head, then lifts her up and sets her on his shoulders. "Ready to go for a ride, Joey-Roo?"

Rose is whining a little and rubbing her eyes, so Calder swings her up onto his shoulders too. "Let's go, Rose."

As the guys zoom along the beach and into the surf, while holding their hands protectively on their daughter's backs, the girls squeal their excitement and grab onto their fathers' hair. Talia nods toward our husbands' crazy antics. "Aren't you glad they never grew up, Cass?"

I watch my husband being such a wonderful father to Rose, and think about our second child growing inside me. I'm nervous and hopeful, but I've never felt safer or more loved. "I'm thankful every single day, but..." I pause and hold out my pinky, wrinkling my nose. "Let's not tell them that."

Talia snags my pinky with hers and we laugh at our husbands being big kids, while absolutely adoring the wonderful, big-hearted men we fell in love with.

"Oh, there was a beer buried in the bottom," Talia says a few minutes later. "I'm going to take it to Sebastian."

I look at her in surprise. "I thought he doesn't drink?"

"It's incredibly rare." Standing, she nods. "This one beer will probably be all he has all week."

When she walks away, I close my eyes for a minute, surprised at how tired I am.

A shadow suddenly blocks the sun and I open my eyes to see Calder standing in front of me. "Are you feeling okay?"

"Yeah, just a little tired. It could be the sun too. That always wears me out. Where's Rose?"

He turns his head and I follow his line of sight, laughing to see both girls clinging to Sebastian's long legs like strips of Velcro as he walks with giant steps in and out of the surf. "She's in good hands. Speaking of which..."

He holds his hand out and I instantly take it. I'm pulled to my feet and Calder spins me into his arms, then twirls me away. "Are we dancing?" I ask, enjoying this playful side of my husband.

Tugging me back into his arms, he turns me around so our backs are to our family. As we slowly sway to the ocean's rhythmic waves, he rests his hand on my belly and whispers in my ear, "We're making memories, Raven mine."

* * *

Thank you for reading **BLOOD ROSE! If you found BLOOD ROSE** an entertaining and enjoyable read, I hope you'll consider taking the time to leave a review and share your thoughts in the online bookstore where you purchased it. Your review could be the one to help another reader decide to read **BLOOD ROSE** and the other books in the **IN THE SHADOWS** series!

Coming up next is NOBLE BRIT (IN THE SHADOWS, Book 9). Turn the page to see the cover and summary.

NOBLE BRIT

The last thing I need is to be assigned as Mina Blake's bodyguard. I'm too blunt, too experienced, and too damned jaded to treat the coddled heiress like the men in the Blake family do.

She has never known tough love.

Until me.

Dear Readers: **NOBLE BRIT** *is a stand alone story in the IN THE SHADOWS series, but if you haven't read the previous books in the series, you'll miss out on seeing Mina and Den's interactions with the Blake family and learning why they deserve their own happy-ever-after.*

DID you know there are **audiobooks** for the **IN THE SHADOWS** series? The audiobooks bring these stories to a whole new level. You can listen to samples and check them out on Amazon and iTunes.

TO KEEP up-to-date when the next P.T. Michelle book will release, join my free newsletter http://bit.ly/11tqAQN . An email will come straight to your inbox on the day a new book releases.

OTHER BOOKS BY P.T. MICHELLE

In the Shadows

(Contemporary Romance, 18+)

Mister Black (Book 1 - Talia & Sebastian, Part 1)

Scarlett Red (Book 2 - Talia & Sebastian, Part 2)

Blackest Red (Book 3 - Talia & Sebastian, Part 3)

Gold Shimmer (Book 4 - Cass & Calder, Part 1)

Steel Rush (Book 5 - Cass & Calder, Part 2)

Black Platinum (Book 6 - Talia & Sebastian, Stand Alone Novel)

Reddest Black (Book 7 - Talia & Sebastian, Stand Alone Novel)

Blood Rose (Book 8 - Cass & Calder, Stand Alone Novel)

Noble Brit (Book 9 - Mina & Den, Stand Alone Novel - Coming March 2019)

Note: Mister Black is the only novella. All the other books are novel length.

Brightest Kind of Darkness Series

(YA/New Adult Paranormal Romance, 16+)

Ethan (Prequel)
Brightest Kind of Darkness (Book 1)
Lucid (Book 2)
Destiny (Book 3)
Desire (Book 4)
Awaken (Book 5)

Other works by P.T. Michelle writing as Patrice Michelle

Bad in Boots series
(Contemporary Romance, 18+)

Harm's Hunger
Ty's Temptation
Colt's Choice
Josh's Justice

Kendrian Vampires series
(Paranormal Romance, 18+)

A Taste for Passion
A Taste for Revenge
A Taste for Control

Stay up-to-date on her latest releases:

Join P.T's Newsletter:
http://bit.ly/11tqAQN

Visit P.T. :

Website: http://www.ptmichelle.com

Twitter: https://twitter.com/PT_Michelle

Facebook:
https://www.facebook.com/PTMichelleAuthor

Instagram: http://instagram.com/p.t.michelle

Goodreads:
http://www.goodreads.com/author/show/4862274.P_T_Michelle

P.T. Michelle's Facebook Readers' Group:
https://www.facebook.com/groups/PTMichelleReadersGroup/

ACKNOWLEDGEMENTS

To my truly awesome beta readers: Joey Berube, Amy Bensette, and Magen Chambers, you ladies are so wonderful to read so quickly and come back with such great notes on **BLOOD ROSE**. You always help make my books the best they can be!

To my fabulous critique partner, Trisha Wolfe, thank you for reading **BLOOD ROSE** at the speed of light! You're such a great sounding board and give fabulous feedback!

To my family, thank you for understanding the time and effort each book takes. I love you all and truly appreciate your unending support.

To my amazing fans, thank you so much for your love and support of my IN THE SHADOWS series and characters! Every time you post a review or tell your reader friends about the series, more people discover my series. Which means there will be even more readers to discuss the books with. I appreciate you all so much!

ABOUT THE AUTHOR

P.T. Michelle is the *NEW YORK TIMES*, *USA TODAY*, and International bestselling author of the contemporary romance series IN THE SHADOWS, the YA/New Adult crossover series BRIGHTEST KIND OF DARKNESS, and the romance series: BAD IN BOOTS, KENDRIAN VAMPIRES and SCIONS (listed under Patrice Michelle). She keeps a spiral notepad with her at all times, even on her nightstand. When P.T. isn't writing, she can usually be found reading or taking pictures of landscapes, sunsets and anything beautiful or odd in nature.

To keep up-to-date when the next P.T. Michelle book will release, join P.T.'s free newsletter.

www.ptmichelle.com

CPSIA information can be obtained
at www.ICGtesting.com
Printed in the USA
LVHW091300130221
679237LV00026B/201